A NIGHT I

Sajjad Zaheer (1905–1973) was a towering intellectual figure in twentieth-century India. One of the founders of the All-India Progressive Writers' Association (AIPWA), his writings span a variety of genres and his ideas traverse national boundaries. As a political leader, writer, translator, poet and journalist, Zaheer engaged with many of the pressing issues of his day. *A Night in London* is his most important literary work.

Bilal Hashmi is a Henry M. MacCracken fellow in the Department of Comparative Literature at New York University.

A NIGHT IN LONDON

Sajjad Zaheer

Translated by
Bilal Hashmi

HARPER**PERENNIAL**

NEW YORK • LONDON • TORONTO • SYDNEY • NEW DELHI • AUCKLAND

HARPER**PERENNIAL**

First published in English in India in 2011 by Harper Perennial
An imprint of HarperCollins *Publishers* India
a joint venture with
The India Today Group

ISBN: 978-93-5029-088-0

2 4 6 8 10 9 7 5 3 1

HarperCollins *Publishers*
A-53, Sector 57, Noida 201301, India
77-85 Fulham Palace Road, London W6 8JB, United Kingdom
Hazelton Lanes, 55 Avenue Road, Suite 2900, Toronto, Ontario M5R 3L2
and 1995 Markham Road, Scarborough, Ontario M1B 5M8, Canada
25 Ryde Road, Pymble, Sydney, NSW 2073, Australia
31 View Road, Glenfield, Auckland 10, New Zealand
10 East 53rd Street, New York NY 10022, USA

Typeset in 11.5/14.5 Bodoni MT at
SŪRYA

Printed and bound at
Thomson Press (India) Ltd.

FOREWORD

This book can hardly be called a novel or a story.
Read it if you wish to see one aspect of the life of
Indian students in Europe.

Most of it was written in London and Paris, and on
board a ship during my return journey to India. That
was more than two years ago. When I read through
this manuscript now, I feel reluctant to have it
published.

It is one thing to sit down in Paris at the culmination
of several years of study in Europe and, under the
spell of private emotional conflict, to write a book of
a hundred to a hundred-and-fifty pages. But to have
spent two-and-a-half years since then taking part in
the revolutionary movement of workers and peasants
in India, breathing in unison with millions of people
and listening to the beating of their hearts, is entirely
another matter.

Today I could not write a book of this kind; nor
would I consider it necessary to write it.

Wazir Manzil, Lucknow   SAJJAD ZAHEER
15 September 1938

TRANSLATOR'S ACKNOWLEDGEMENTS

This translation is based in the main on the critical edition of Mohammad Feroz (Delhi: Saqi Book Depot, 2001), though I have consulted as many versions of the text as were available to me. Where there were inconsistencies, I have occasionally given priority to the most recent edition published by National Book Trust, India (New Delhi, 2005). Over the last several years, the world of Urdu letters has witnessed a growing body of secondary literature on Zaheer. I have availed myself of this, as well as of an impressive tribute to Zaheer edited by the late Ali Baquer (New Delhi: Afro-Asian Writers' Association, 1987), which remains the most comprehensive introduction to the author in English.

I am indebted to a number of people who assisted me in the completion of this translation. When dictionaries and much else failed, I benefitted from the sound advice of my parents, Romana and Jameel; and it is to them that I express my deepest gratitude. Carlo Coppola lent his critical eye to the manuscript in all its iterations, and was most generous in sharing his wealth of knowledge about Zaheer and the Progressive Writers' Association. I must also record my thanks to several persons who helped and encouraged me in various ways, foremost among them Ashley Cohen, Aamir Mufti, C.M. Naim, Tim Reiss, Daisy Rockwell and Kristin Ross. At an early stage of the translation, I was warmly aided by the encouragement—not to mention communism—of Ralph Russell, who regrettably did not live to see it in print. Najma Zaheer Baquer and Seema Baquer both went over the entire manuscript and provided crucial feedback along the way; I remain grateful for their patience and support. My editors Prema Govindan and Shantanu Ray Chaudhuri dealt expertly with a difficult text. Needless to say, all errors remain my own.

BILAL HASHMI

1

London is cloaked in a swollen, thick fog, yellowish, dense, dark; a blanket of sorts, it is at once damp and cold, covering the entire body, especially the nose and mouth. It is difficult to breathe, and when you do, you feel as though you are inhaling a wet mist. Everything is damp. Tiny droplets of water have collected everywhere. It is not terribly cold, but even this is quite painful. It is afternoon, though it seems that night has set in. No gleam in the street lights. It appears as if a struggle is raging between darkness and light. The occasional clearing of the fog makes the gaslights flare up.

Despite the weather, London does not lack activity. Shops are well lit, and the streets are crammed with cars, lorries and buses. On the pavement, where people walk, those leaving their offices—secretaries, clerks, businessmen, typists, students, and men and women working in factories—scurry past. It is now six o'clock, and London's students, 'intellectuals'—the 'genuine and the fake'—and those who come to visit England from all nations of the world stop over at Bloomsbury. This is where England's revolutionary thinkers, artists, expatriates, writers, and all such people who are suspended in a mental void gather, creating a peculiar atmosphere.

It is now ten past six. Azam repeatedly glances at the clock in the Russell Square underground station.

———

It looks as though the wretch will break her promise again and won't show up. This isn't the first time. I'm beginning to feel embarrassed at my own condition. I know all too well that she doesn't have the least bit of affection for me. And it's *I* who can't stop pursuing her. After all, there are lots of other women in London. And I'm not that hideous either. But I'm so weak; I don't have any control over myself. How many times have I meant to stop seeing her altogether, to stop talking to her. And how many times have I told myself that if I meet her on the street, I'd look the other way? And if she came to meet me on her own, I'd say to her straight out: 'Leave me alone. If you don't love me, why did you come to me? Find another lover. You have lots of other admirers. I hate you.' And a host of equally harsh and fierce declarations, which would surely wound her heart and bring her pain and torment. This way, I'd have my revenge. The anxiety, grief, confusion, indignation, jealousy, malice, anger, sorrow that I feel because of her—I could avenge all of it.

But I have never been successful. Once, she had promised to meet me on a Saturday evening, saying that after her office got over at six, she would go home and reach my place by seven, seven-thirty. Seven-thirty to eight o'clock, eight to nine, and nine to ten—I couldn't even go out and have dinner. And I kept waiting and waiting. At ten o'clock there was a knock on the door. I was so filled with anger that I didn't even say, 'Yes, come in.' The door opened. Who? Not her, but the maid. 'Mr Azam, someone would like to speak to you on the phone.' It felt for a moment as though all the blood in my body rushed to my head—warm, warm blood.

I said, 'Thank you, Mary,' and went to answer the telephone.

'Who is it?' I asked, even though I knew.

'It's me, darling. Sweetheart, are you very cross with me? I can tell from your voice. Do forgive me, but it isn't my fault. Some people came over to meet us. My mother insisted that I look after the guests. I tried very hard to come up with an excuse, but to no avail, and now it's too late. My darling Azam, forgive me.'

My anger knew no bounds. I hadn't seen her for a week. Something new would come up every day; and today, when she was finally set to meet me, this was how she dashed my longings and desires. I was inclined to say 'Go to hell' and hang up, thereby ending the discussion: a discussion that was taking place using wires; a discussion in which the human voice, detaching itself from the human body, transforms merely into a *voice*, striking our ears as the epitome of sincerity and, to some extent, taking on the guise of revelation. Revelation, though, is a heavenly 'reality'. But over the telephone, it's terribly difficult to distinguish between truth and falsehood: it's a brilliant tool for lying. Surely, she was telling lies—guests came over! She could have made up some excuse, and her mother would have let her go; she would certainly have let her. She is lying to me; she is making excuses. She must have gone out with someone else who caught her fancy. She must have gone out on a date with him to the cinema, the theatre, or on a car ride. I don't even own a car; nor am I wealthy. That is why she hasn't come, and now she's just making excuses. 'Azam, darling, my beloved Azam.' Liar, impostor. All these thoughts swirled around in my head, but I responded, 'Really? And I'm half-dead waiting for you. You could have at least called up a little earlier. But it's not that late. The underground and buses run till twelve-thirty. You can spend an hour and a half with me . . .'

Instead of rising with anger, my voice began to tremble; I could sense it. I felt that I was debasing myself, but a force—in the face of which I became completely powerless and submissive—was dragging me towards further humiliation. In order to retain my self-respect, I began to think of how the torment one withstands in love doesn't count as torment. I began to recall the complaints and lamentations of the vast majority of Urdu poets who become dogs in the street of their beloved, are kicked around by their rivals, bear the insults of the doorkeeper, and not only endure their beloved's blandishments and whims, but welcome these as a pleasure to the soul—so much so that mountains of injustice and oppression would crumble before them.

But poetry is one thing, and the reality of degradation quite another. I fancied myself to be tough, but time and time again, the shameful face of rejection appears before my eyes.

She replied, 'No, Azam darling. It is too late now; I need to get up early in the morning, you already know that . . .'

'But tomorrow's Sunday. You don't need to go to work.'

'That's true, but even then, you know the maid arrives late on Sunday, and I need to help my mother with the chores. Really, I'm telling the truth . . . It seems you don't believe what I'm saying . . . This isn't an excuse. You know how much I love you! All right; I'll call you tomorrow around noon and decide on a time to meet you. Please forgive me this time.'

She hasn't got a moment to speak to me on the telephone now and then has to wake up early tomorrow to help her mother. Lies, lies—she's surely been going out on dates with someone else. In my heart, I can feel this is the moment I have been waiting for, that I would have no better opportunity and that I should reveal all my doubts to her; but I replied, 'All right, Jean. I'll wait for your call at noon tomorrow. Good night.'

The next day, the telephone remained silent. My day was wasted. If Rao hadn't shown up close to one o'clock, I'd surely have gone crazy. Rao is a lucky man. No one has ever seen him get entangled in the web of love, but he always seems to have an attractive girl around.

How much longer shall I wait here? It's a quarter past six. It's cold and there's still no sign of Jean.

——

But Jean's smiling face, her long, slender body, her sparkling eyes that worriedly darted from here to there, the sound of her laughter, her getting anxious and then lying—all of it flashed in Azam's head like lightning and, for short periods of time, numbed his brain. Every other minute, the door of the underground's lift would open and people would get out. Twenty, sometimes thirty. More than that on some occasions, less at others. And when the last person got out and he couldn't find Jean, Azam grew more anxious. He peered at the clock, and looked at the people milling about, waiting for the next train. Large advertisements hung near the newspaper stand: the *Times*, *Daily Mail*, *Morning Post*, *Daily Telegraph*, and so forth. Azam's glance fell upon the evening newspapers being sold outside the station.

'Results of the football match! Final match results!'

the newspaper vendors were shouting. In the meantime, his gaze fell upon a number of headlines that were plastered on signboards.

MEETING OF UNEMPLOYED WORKERS IN HYDE PARK.

10 BRITISH SOLDIERS PREVENT 10,000 INDIAN NATIVES FROM CREATING DISTURBANCE—1 WHITE INJURED, 15 NATIVES DEAD.

These advertisements were emblazoned in red letters on large spools of paper two-and-a-half feet long and about a foot wide. Azam's thoughts shifted for a moment from waiting for his girlfriend to India, his country. The disdain with which these wretched English newspapers call us natives! We're 'natives', and the red-faced monkeys who live in *this* country, who are *they*?

Azam's thoughts would not extend to the unfortunate poor who faced the bullets of the white man and the unemployed English workers in Hyde Park who died hungry.

An Arabic saying goes: 'Waiting is more painful than death'. Faced with the prospect of death, a person's senses become confounded. Similarly, the intensity of waiting prevents the brain from working. This is especially true in the case of the anticipation which Azam was experiencing. He had even begun to forget Jean's expected arrival. Jean's coming, their meeting, happiness; her not coming and the sadness that would follow: all these thoughts and feelings escaped their material reality and adopted a faint and meaningless aspect, and a dark cloud cast itself upon his mind.

'Hello, Azam! What are you doing standing here?' called out Rao, slapping Azam's shoulder upon emerging from the underground station.

Rao's sudden appearance put Azam at ease. In the same way that the soul, in moments of grief and torment, is made lighter by crying, Azam's thoughts, which were stuck on one point and ached like a wound, were diverted. Rao was his friend. At the same time, Azam wasn't sure what explanation he should offer. It was, after all, *not* a matter of great pride that Mr Azam was braving the cold, waiting for Jean at the Russell Square station, with no sign of the beloved. But Azam thought that there was no point hiding the facts from Rao. He was sure to see through the situation.

And so he answered while attempting a grin: 'I was supposed to meet Jean. She promised to meet me here at six. She hasn't come yet. It's now twenty minutes past six. There's a party at Naim's place tonight; he has invited both of us. I don't know what to do.'

Rao's thoughts did not venture in the direction of Azam's inner turmoil. Was it really something to get worried about if someone did not arrive as planned? Especially a girl? The poor thing must have had a problem getting dressed. She was probably not satisfied with the shade of her lipstick and was trying to find the right one. Or, perhaps she got delayed while adjusting the angle of her hat. There could be hundreds of reasons for being late. It was hardly the sort of thing to get all angry and restless over.

But Rao, after all, was not Jean's lover. It was Azam who was smitten with her.

Rao exclaimed, 'What! You've been invited to Naim's place as well? He has invited me too. Let's go together. Jean knows Naim's address. She'll reach there straight. Why stay out here in the cold and freeze? Come, let's go.'

Azam hesitated for a moment. Should I wait or not? Maybe she'll get here in five minutes. If I leave now, waiting all this while would have been pointless. And maybe she won't show up at all—who knows, he thought.

Rao saw the conflict raging within Azam. In his Madrasi drawl, he quickly repeated, 'Do come now, Azam. What's the point in sticking around? It's not as though she'll go back home if she doesn't find you here. If she wants to come, she can certainly come right to Naim's place.'

Azam decided that it was better to go with Rao. The thought that he had lost his self-respect in pursuit of that woman swept over him once again and the heavy load of degradation began settling on his heart. His feet began moving, but slowly, and he walked out of the station with Rao.

Rao glanced at his friend's face, which was as lifeless as a wounded animal's: pain and helplessness, dread and frailty stamped on it. Rao suddenly understood his companion's predicament. He felt embarrassed at not being able to put his finger on Azam's real condition until now. He was filled with sympathy for Azam. Then came pity, and with it laughter. That girl has rendered a perfectly normal, agreeable person crazy. For half an hour, this poor fellow's been waiting and there's not even a hint that she will show up. Today is not the first time. Now Azam's studies, too, have begun to be affected by her. If the situation remains as it is now, it will become difficult for him to clear his exams. Were there some way to get her away from Azam, it would be all for the better, he thought.

'Oh, enough, Bhai Azam. Don't be so depressed. Jean will surely show up soon enough. Something must have delayed her. The fog's so intense today, and so is the cold. One dreads leaving home. Come on, let's go to the pub. We'll drink a glass of beer and then head to Naim's place.'

Azam's will power had vanished by now. 'Yes, certainly,' he replied softly. 'Why not drink a peg of whisky or brandy in this cold?' Rao and Azam continued walking slowly. The fog cleared for a few minutes, causing the gas lights to glow. Rao had a dark face and large, egg-shaped eyes like those of Rajput princes in old portraits. He was of medium stature and, like most Hindu gods, of delicate body. He had soft, silky black hair which fell on his forehead. His face glowed with intelligence but it appeared as though he possessed a certain weakness of character. Whenever his face came into view under the light, it was plain to see that he was grieving over Azam's condition.

Azam fixed his gaze on Rao's countenance. He realized immediately that Rao was expressing sympathy for him, not through words but with his demeanour and his silence. Azam was somewhat relieved. There were a great many things in the world besides love.

———

'Did you see this evening's paper? There was shooting in India again,' Azam said.

'No, I didn't; but I saw the headline. It's becoming commonplace now. The lives of us black men are no better than insects and vermin, and the fault most probably lies with us! We Indians—vulgar, wretched, shameless—deserve this. We get kicked around by them but aren't satisfied with serving the British. The Hindu is waiting for a chance to kill the Muslim; the Muslim is ready to strangle the Hindu. Forget gunfire. If it were up to me, I'd put the entire nation in the mouth of a cannon and blow it up. It doesn't even have the right to exist. Think of it: less than a hundred thousand British happily rule over thirty-five million people. And rule—what kind of rule! In India, the status of even the lowliest of the low Englishmen is far superior to the most distinguished of distinguished Indians. Even if here, in England, Englishmen polish our shoes, and Englishwomen fall

in love with us, all of us—"black people", "natives"—
are thought of as worse than slaves east of Suez. I can
become a barrister, and you an engineer, but in India
we'll remain "natives". And we'll suffer the kicks of
the British. And in spite of this, you'll turn around
yet again and address them as "master", "lord" and
"daddy". If, after being denigrated to such an extent,
a nation can't feel the lice crawling over its ears, it's
better for it to be wiped off the face of the earth. I'm
happy when news of gunfire comes from India,' said
Rao bitterly.

Azam began chuckling at Rao's diatribe. He did
not have much interest in politics, but Rao's words
had such fervour that they affected him.

'Rao, my dear chap, why exaggerate so? It's easy
to talk, but no one's ready to help the people who are
working for the progress of the nation. If you really
feel so strongly about India ridding itself of its
debasement, why don't you go and work with those
people who are striving for the betterment of the
nation?'

'Striving for the betterment of the nation? Do tell
me what that means,' said Rao quickly. 'No one
knows what exactly "the betterment of the nation"
means, let alone striving for it! Is there betterment in
store for the nation in weaving like a woman? Or does
it lie in becoming like Mahatma Gandhi and searching
for truth? Or in council membership and the ministry?
Or in taking part in social reform or untouchables'
conferences? Is there betterment for the nation in

government service? In joining the Hindu Mahasabha
or the Muslim League? Everyone has a prescription
for the betterment of the nation; it seems as though
every mother's son is struggling for the betterment of
the nation. Every person cries out and says that he's
working for the betterment of the nation. It has
reached its limit. The British government's watchdog
is convinced that it, too, wants what's best for the
nation. And what *is* the condition of the nation? On
the one hand is the shadow of poverty and hunger; on
the other, a web of oppression and force. These are
suffocating us. How wonderful these people who are
doing what is good for us are; I've had enough of *that*
kind of goodness. At least I don't deceive people; I
admit openly that I want only what's good for me;
never mind the nation and notions of helping it. Mr
Azam, India's condition has crossed the limit. The
sooner the nation called India perishes, the better.'

'You should go kill yourself, Rao. I've never seen a
more cynical person than you. But you seem so
happy. It's a strange thing,' replied Azam. And then
his thoughts went back to Jean, and he became
aware of his desperation again. He suddenly turned
quiet, and, once more, sadness became apparent on
his face.

Rao immediately sensed this change in Azam and
answered jokingly: 'The secret to leading a happy life
lies in hopelessness. Its loftiest degree is the condition
of senselessness. This is the state in which a person
can no longer see the difference between happiness

and sadness, comfort and pain. This is what we
Hindus call Nirvana.'

Sorrow had once again cast its spell upon Azam. He
tried to laugh at Rao's words, but only managed a
meaningless smile. Why didn't Jean show up? Does
she not love me at all? But then he thought, if that
were true, why would she promise to show up? Why
would she declare her love? Were those lies? All her
words of love and affection? The giant of suspicion
and envy began taking control of Azam's mind once
again. Who knows, maybe she has a number of
lovers. These days, that's not considered a bad thing
here. She comes and visits me once a week, and then
perhaps there's someone besides me as well. All this
probably because she thinks that telling me bluntly
that she doesn't love me will hurt me. With this in
mind, she wants to maintain the status quo.
Eventually, she will distance herself and won't come
to see me at all. To delay like this, and not show up
after promising to do so, is a portent of this.

The fog swept down once more, and darkness filled
the air. Rao pulled up the collar of his coat, lowered
his shoulders and, placing both hands firmly inside
his pockets, began walking briskly.

'Come on, let's walk a little faster. I'm cold,' said
Rao.

Azam offered no response but quickened his pace.
Within a few minutes they arrived at the pub and
went inside.

2

Pubs in England are generally divided into two or three sections: the section immediately on entering, where the working class goes, and the inner section, which is usually occupied by those with money. Sometimes, there is also a third section for those who are in a hurry and need to have a drink. This section has no stools for the patrons. The bartender stands in the middle and is surrounded on all sides by a wooden table, which is about a yard and a half long and about a foot wide. Towards the interior of this table are taps from which glasses are filled with beer and given to those who do not wish to drink from bottles.

This was an ordinary pub. Two or three benches were laid out in the section for the poor and in front of them stood a wooden table. A few workers were sitting on the benches, each with a glass of beer; three or four of them were standing at the corner of the table. The bartender had just placed a full glass from which foam was spilling over in front of someone; another's glass was half-empty and he was smoking

15

his pipe in silence; yet another's glass had been drained out and he was asking for more. Tobacco smoke filled the room.

Rao and Azam entered this room, approached the corner of the bar and stood there.

'Good evening, sir!' called out the owner-cum-bartender, spotting Rao. Since Rao frequented this pub, its proprietor had begun to recognize him.

'The weather's terrible,' the owner said immediately after his greeting. In England, everyone considers it his duty to express an opinion about the weather. Instead of enquiring about how one is, it has become a custom of sorts to mention how good or bad the weather is, in response to which the other person concurs; and if the first person has nothing important to say, but does not wish to remain quiet either, the discussion on the weather would resume. Every individual conveys his practical knowledge on the matter. Last year, the weather was not so bad; during the summer five years ago the sun could not be seen at all, and it rained continuously; and in winter there was nothing but sunshine; it was so cold thirty years ago that the water froze in taps and people had taken to skating on the Thames, and so on and so forth. In short, the sort of discussion that never ends. The British have most likely invented this custom in order to preserve their privacy. By talking about the weather, they prevent others from discussing personal affairs. The weather is the sort of subject on which every individual can express an opinion with freedom, without revealing his name, place of birth, occupation, salary, religion and caste, as is customary in our country.

'Good evening!' replied Rao. 'Yes, the weather is terrible. I don't know when this fog will lift.' And then he asked Azam: 'What'll you have?'

'Brandy,' replied Azam. He wanted something strong.

Rao ordered a brandy for Azam and a whiskey for himself. The bartender placed both glasses and a bottle of soda before Azam and Rao. Rao, after adding soda, and Azam, without mixing it in, lifted their glasses to their lips.

'Cheerio, Azam!' said Rao with a smile and took his first gulp.

'Cheerio, Rao,' replied Azam softly, in a sorrowful voice, and sipped the drink. Then they placed their glasses on the table. It seemed as though both were attempting to start a conversation—Azam, to forget his present condition; and Rao, who was increasingly feeling the effect of Azam's dejection, to comfort Azam in some way. But, as is often the case, conversation does not happen when you try. A painful, heavy silence settled between them, made all the more pronounced by the fact that they were drinking. Instead of reviving their spirits, the alcohol had the opposite effect.

Jean, Jean, Jean! It was as though someone were pounding a hammer inside Azam's head.

Rao himself was now so absorbed in Azam's

condition that his friend's pain had begun tormenting him too. This grief isn't the sort that gives someone strength at the end, thought Rao. This is a completely futile, profitless torment; its outcome is nothing other than the pain of the heart and mind. All afflictions are not fruitless. Some give us mental and physical benefit; or if not us, then our suffering may yield benefit to someone else.

Before Rao's eyes there suddenly appears a procession of Indians, most of them poor, shabbily dressed people, on whose faces the effect of sun, wind and hunger had etched wrinkles and craters; whose hands, it appears, have become hard and strong from labour, whose eyes have the light of toil in them, whose shoulders are hunched, and whose stick-like legs protrude from their soiled dhotis.

A crowd of these people on the stretch of the road. Part of this procession are Indian students and those poor who now cannot even find a job that pays twenty-five rupees a month: thin and emaciated, with weak chests, a four-day stubble, a tiny English coat and dhoti, dirty spectacles, bare-headed, these too in their hundreds, and many others of the same class. The entire mass is moving, in ocean-like undulations. They try to make their way forward, but the path is blocked. The whites are standing in front with rifles. Machine guns as well. Bayonets glisten in the sun. Behind the soldiers are English officers mounted on horses. Intense sunshine, heat, beads of sweat on faces. The wind has ceased. Rao is standing in the middle of the congregation. But why aren't we moving forward? What's the point in stopping when we've come so far? Cries of 'move forward, move forward' suddenly reach his ears and a wave of happiness runs through his body.

Torment that is beneficial; torment that ushers in relief. We have come this far with great difficulty and are poised to move further ahead. But no. No. No. No. Life is not as simple as we think . . .

He stands alone in an open field; the entire crowd has disappeared. The whites stand in front, and on all four sides, here and there, are bloodstains—warm, fresh blood. And wounded people and corpses. Someone lies face-down on the ground, hands pressed under his stomach; another flat on his back, shot in the head—terror-stricken eyes fluttering involuntarily, mouth agape. On his face, neck, and soiled kurta are large red bloodstains. A wounded person, shot in the foot, screams from the intensity of his pain. *This* is torment. This is what is called pain. Just take a look at this glass of whiskey, will you. It has lost its vigour, its coolness; its colour has changed, a dark viscous thing, a deep red colour. Blood, warm fresh blood. Oh God!

10 BRITISH SOLDIERS PREVENT 10,000 INDIAN NATIVES FROM CREATING DISTURBANCE—1 WHITE INJURED, 15 NATIVES DEAD.

All of a sudden, Rao felt cold and he began to shiver. He lifted his glass and, in one gulp, downed the

ng whiskey. He glanced towards Azam, who,
.ad emptied his glass. Azam asked Rao, 'How
.t another?'

'I don't know,' replied Rao. 'I'm not feeling very
well today. I didn't eat anything this afternoon and
had just one cup during teatime. I wasn't hungry
then. Now that I've had alcohol on an empty stomach,
my head is beginning to spin.'

'Oh, wow!' Azam blurted with a laugh. 'You have
the strength for just *one* glass? Come on, have a
drink; it's not like you'll die if you drink more. Get
something to eat after you leave and you'll be fine.'

'Very well, then,' relented Rao. 'Fine, if you insist.
Come, let's have another.' Azam ordered two more
glasses, and both friends resumed drinking in silence.

'You wouldn't happen to have a light, would ye?'
Standing next to Rao was an English worker who
had asked him the question in an accent peculiar to
that class. Rao turned around, glanced at the man,
pulled a box of matches from his pocket and placed
it in the worker's hand. The man began to light his
pipe. The burning light of the match fell on his face.
He was a heavily-built man, between forty and forty-
five; a small moustache hung over his lips, its corners
moist with beer. A deep rosy colour; a slightly swollen
nose. Small eyes, but there was a sharpness in them;
light-brown eyebrows; medium stature; a fairly stout
body; hands with plump fingers. The man's clothes, a
dark almond-like colour, were old and completely
tattered, a patch on his trousers near the knee. As he

returned Rao's box of matches, he declared, 'There's chaos all across India.'

Hearing this, Azam said to himself: And what's it to *you*? We're not interested. Why bother with small talk! For God's sake, leave me alone. Right now I don't have time to look into the reasons behind India's chaos. Jean. Jean. Axes were still grinding inside his head. He remained silent.

And Rao thought: Why would this person want to speak with us? What interest would *he* have in India? He probably thinks of us as slaves and hates us. His own condition is so bad . . . but like most Englishmen, he probably thinks of India, *our* nation, as *his* personal property. There's gunfire in India. *His* people have opened fired on *our* people. They consider it their duty to spread civilization and maintain peace and tranquility throughout the world by opening fire and showering bombs from the sky. And this fellow wants to have a discussion with me? What would he have to say?

He answered the Englishman: 'Yes, bad news from India, but I couldn't care the least bit. The more unstable India becomes, the happier I am.' A statement brimming with anger and sarcasm.

But Rao's tone had little effect on the portly worker. He took a puff from his pipe and then, in a voice devoid of any emotion, replied, 'I'll certainly say that I don't enjoy hearin' news of fightin', chaos and bloodshed. And when us English can't rule India without the help of an army, I say,' raising his voice

a little, he repeated, 'I say it's time for us to pack our
bags and go home, and surrender the country to the
Indians; they can take back their country and do
with it whatever they want. In any case, I could
never bear Germany, France or any other nation
comin' to rule over England. So what right do we
have of stayin' in India?' He turned in the other
direction and, addressing the worker next to him,
said, 'Jim, what I say is right, isn't it?'

Jim, who was tall and thin and had prominent
cheekbones, was listening attentively to his companion,
Tom. With his head lowered, he was eyeing his glass
of beer. He offered no response at first. The hint of
resentment that Rao had for Tom now turned into
interest. These English workers aren't on the whole as
foolish as England's newspapers. There's still a little
room left for truth in their hearts. But Rao became
angry again. Then why don't they *do* something! Rao
glanced at Jim, now waiting for his response.

Tom said to Jim again: 'Well, Jim. What's your
opinion?'

'Tom!' replied Jim in a whisper. 'But if we leave
India, where would that country be? We read in the
papers that Hindus and Muslims are two different
faiths, and that there's always been fighting between
'em. They're sworn enemies. If we don't keep peace in
India and leave the country and come back home,
there'll be lots of bloodshed.'

Tom lifted his glass, downed all his beer in two
gulps, and shouted, 'Jim, listen. Before the war, I was

in India and I saw the conditions there. I was young then, I was an idiot—do you hear me?—I was an idiot. The mere thought of the British Empire made the blood rush through my veins. I'd call Indians "darkies", "niggers", an' "natives"; I'd think of Indians as worse than animals. That's what was taught to us in the army. I myself have seen how we instil peace in Indians! I tell you, Jim, the basis of our rule in India is *fear*. You say there's peace in India because of us. Maybe, but peace at what cost? I've seen with my own eyes the poor, naked, hungry, who live like insects and vermin—hundreds of thousands, millions of people. It'd be difficult for you to call 'em people. I tell you the truth when I say that the condition of unemployed workers here's a thousand times better. And still, there's a lot of uproar, a meeting every other day here; marches are held, and the government's warned that until it makes arrangements for the livelihoods of unemployed workers, it doesn't deserve to be called civilized. Believe what I'm sayin', Jim. With my own eyes, I've seen poverty and only poverty from one corner of India to the other. We've been there for more than a hundred and fifty years and have maintained peace and quiet! I've no patience when you speak to me of maintainin' peace!'

Tom's words had an effect on Jim, but there was still some doubt left in his mind. It was possible that Tom was exaggerating. 'You've been to India, Tom. You've seen the conditions there. Whatever I know about India is from the papers . . . and,' Jim said with some hesitation, 'it's always written in the papers that if our government doesn't stay in India, chaos and fightin' will spread throughout that country. I don't know anything,' said Jim, shaking his head.

'You read that in the *papers*.' Tom was now fairly intoxicated. Argument aroused even more fervour in him. 'Jim!' he cried, slapping his hand on Jim's shoulder. 'You silly bloke! Have you lost your senses?' Hearing this, those standing nearby took their glasses, approached Tom and Jim, and formed a circle around them. Everyone wanted to be part of the discussion.

Tom continued to speak. 'You say that you read all these things in the papers, and that's why you don't believe what I say. All right then, tell me this: Is all that the papers write about *us* true? Whenever *we* workers are forced to strike, these papers blame *us*. As if we enjoy bein' poor and get pleasure out of starvin' our wives and children. You wanna call that truth? And when the poor unemployed workers these days gather together and go out on marches to pressure the government and direct the country's attention to their lousy condition, the papers say that they're all petty thieves and good-for-nothings, that we've sold our souls to Moscow. Is *that* true? Tell me, please do. You know my boy; he used to work in a textile factory. He's been unemployed for a year and is sitting idle. He wanders about in the streets in search of work, but he gets the same point-blank refusal wherever he goes. What's he done wrong? If he's given work, he'd teach those people who drive around in big cars how to work. This country has three million people like my boy; our papers call them scoundrels and cripples. And you believe what these sorts of papers have to say. Talk a little sense, Jim!'

Tom's speech left poor Jim completely devastated. The people standing in the vicinity, too, began to nod their heads in agreement with Tom.

Jim responded in a hushed tone, 'You're right, Tom. What you say is right. Believing what these papers say is stupid.'

Tom now began to beam like a child, as though he had won a big victory. He glanced at Rao and Azam and winked with a grin. As if wanting to say: 'Jim's not a lousy sort. His heart's pure. He believes in India's rights. There's just this minor issue he didn't understand, and now he's on our side.'

'Now a glass on me, Jim.' Tom ordered two more glasses: one for himself and the other for Jim. Alcohol makes even the poorest of men generous.

'Thank you, Tom,' said Jim with a smile. The bartender placed two glasses overflowing with beer in front of them. The people in the circle gradually began to drift away. Tom and Jim each took long puffs at the pipe between sips of beer.

Azam thought to himself, I should hurry up. Or Jean might arrive at Naim's place and, not finding me there, leave.

In the meantime, a booming voice was heard from a corner of the room. It appeared that the speaker

was inebriated. 'Hullo, blackies!' he called out to
Azam and Rao. They immediately turned to face
him. Bare-headed, a thin, stricken-looking man with
a tomato-red face was sitting on a bench, cackling a
sottish laugh. Rao and Azam, who were also feeling
the effects of alcohol, trembled with anger.
Humiliation and disgrace are written in the destiny of
Indians. No matter which corner of the world they
are in, it is their lot to be looked upon as slaves. Both
Rao and Azam shared this feeling.

''Ow's Gandy . . . Is's goat well? I was in India. I
was for three years . . . no, no, I was in India for three
years in the army. I saw Calcutta, Delhi, Agra,
Meerut, Peshawar—all of 'em. Ceelcatta's a splendid
city, I 'ad great fun. Gr . . . girls in India are really
great . . . 'Ello, what 'appened? Why's everyone starin'
at me?'

He lifted his glass and downed what little beer was
left in it in a single gulp.

'Another one!' he screamed at the bartender.

The man's yelling caused everyone in the pub to
look his way. The intoxicated English workers were
eyeing him in a manner that made it clear that they
did not appreciate his impolite conduct the least bit.
One had a frown running across his forehead; another
sported a scornful grin.

Azam's face turned red with anger. He did not
know how he would avenge himself on this insolent
drunk. He glared at the drunkard in such a way as to
indicate that if he had his way, he would eat him

alive. The thought of Jean had completely left his mind.

Rao stared at the screamer for some time, then turned his head away and gazed at his glass for some time before whispering, 'Son of a bitch'. Then he lifted his glass and began drinking slowly. His head began to spin a little. White men on bicycles, wearing khaki clothes, were all around him, making a magnificent circle; and he was in the middle, completely alone, a half-empty glass of alcohol in his hand. Thousands upon thousands, multitudes of whites on cycles. Suddenly, it became night, pitch-dark, the only light emanating from the cycle lamps. Rao felt scared. The circle of cycles began to get smaller. The whites on the cycles began to come nearer. They would close in on him within a minute. Oh God! How would he be set free from this curse? He would be crushed in a second. Fear gripped him. His body began to shudder. Hey, hey! He would need to face this trial like a man. He dashed his glass to the floor.

The sound of glass crashing on the floor.

Everyone's gaze fell on Rao.

Rao himself was startled. He looked towards the bartender and said, 'I'm sorry.'

'Not to worry, sir!' he replied with a smile. 'Don't pay attention to this drunk. One glass and his senses are gone. I'm sorry he troubled you fellows.'

The drunkard was now talking to someone else in a loud voice.

Azam turned to Rao. 'It looks as though your

head's spinning. There's too much smoke here. Come,
let's go.'

Both of them moved towards the door. Tom and
Jim had their gazes fixed on them. They looked
towards Azam and Rao smilingly and said, 'Good
evenin'.'

The duo quickly left the pub without responding.
And a sorrowful silence enveloped them.

3

Naimuddin belonged to that group of students who leave India to study in England for a couple of years and end up staying for five or six. Not because they want to trouble their parents unnecessarily and wish to place on them a financial burden greater than what the original duration would have entailed, nor because they are unable to pass their exams owing to their dullness, but because they are infected with the disease of laziness. The same people who prove their mental and physical aptitude in the beginning gradually become lazy after living there for a year or two. They get stuck in England. Students would arrive in London from India and others would return to India from London. But Naimuddin showed no signs of budging.

'Naimuddin, when will you complete your thesis?' people would ask him.

'I'm writing the fifth chapter. It'll be done in a few weeks; and after that I have just another to write. I'll submit it in a month or two.' Naimuddin would always offer this response and, afraid that people

might say that he had given the same answer six
months earlier, would immediately try to change the
subject. 'Have a cigarette,' he would say to the
questioner, presenting him with one. And if he
discerned that the person would not be content without
getting to the heart of the matter, he would say
'Excuse me' and, getting up from his easy chair—
neck lowered, pipe stuffed in mouth, puffing out
smoke like an engine—he would hurry his stout
frame out of the room and escape to the bathroom.
His friends were well-acquainted with this reaction
and would tease him. In the middle of a conversation,
or in front of strangers, whenever Naimuddin spoke
forcefully, as was his habit, someone would ask:
'When will you submit your thesis, Naim?' He would
stop mid-sentence and give the questioner a fretful
glance. 'My thesis is of no interest to anyone here.'
And then he would, feigning unconcern, attempt to
carry on his conversation. His friends would laugh
heartily at this.

Everyone loved Naim as he was always ready to
help others. Even those who were not his friends
would take lawful and unlawful advantage of him. If
one was strapped for cash, he would arrive at Naim's
place to ask for a loan. If someone could not find time
to pay the fees for an examination, he would implore
Naim to go and pay it. If you wanted a free meal,
you would stop over at Naim's place at mealtime. If
someone did not have brand-new novels to read, he
would casually pick up Naim's books and take them

with him. Anyone who wanted to organize a meeting would arrive at Naim's place and have him address invitation envelopes. One whose girlfriend had left him would approach Naim to help him win back her affection.

Naimuddin would always refuse at first: 'Since when do I have the time?', or 'I'm a poor man. Where do I have the money to make a loan?', or 'I have to study right now. That's why I can't do what you want me to'.

But everyone knew that five minutes of pleading was all it would take for Naimuddin to be dragged away from his easy chair—in which he sat from morning till night in his gown, reading a novel—and for him to, for a short while, put aside his laziness to help others.

Naimuddin's room also served as a club for his friends and acquaintances. Every two or three days, six or seven men made it a point to arrive there, and then would ensue a discussion which would last until midnight or the wee hours of the morning. This evening, too, there was a party in Naim's room.

Someone knocked on the door. 'Yes, come in,' responded Naim. He rose from his chair, came near the fireplace and looked towards the door. It opened slowly.

Who could it be? Naim thought to himself. Someone who doesn't come in immediately, but approaches the door and hesitates, as though coming here for the first time . . .

The room was somewhat dark. Only one lamp, covered with a dark red-coloured globe, was lit on a small table in the corner. The fire was burning in the fireplace.

'Won't you come in?' Naim called out again. A woman entered the room. Her features were not clearly visible in the dark—medium stature, delicate body, long black coat and a black hat, the bottom of which drooped over her forehead and eyes, covering her face. She hesitated as she came in. Naimuddin stood surprised and quiet; his eyes were on the person who had arrived. He thought: Who's this getting here so early? And a person I don't even know? But she appears to be refined; not like those who are neither friends nor acquaintances, but still barge into my room.

The woman shut the door behind her and took a couple of steps towards Naim. Now the light was shining fully on her face. The girl isn't bad looking, Naim thought to himself.

'Excuse me,' the girl asked, 'is this Mr Naim's room?'

'I am Naim. Please make yourself comfortable,' replied Naim without moving from near the fireplace. The girl now approached Naim. The full light from the lamp near the chair fell on her face. Her rosy cheeks had become even rosier from the cold; the golden hair, billowing out from under her hat, reached her neck; her large eyes were staring at Naim's face; and the light grin on her lips seemed to betray a sense

of embarrassment. All these made for a strange feeling
in the dim, red light.

She went and stood behind the chair. Only the
large easy chair stood between her and Naim. She
placed both her hands on the chair. Her fingers gave
away her sense of unease and embarrassment; her fist
would half-close and open. But Naim's gaze did not
fall on her hands; he continued looking at her in
wonderment.

'Mr Rao told me that there was to be a party at
your place this evening. He promised to meet me
here, between six-thirty and seven o'clock, but it
seems he hasn't arrived yet.'

The girl uttered this in a slightly apologetic tone, as
though she was ashamed, thinking herself to be an
uninvited guest at the home of someone she did not
even know.

'Yes, yes!' said Naim quickly. 'Please feel at home.
Rao must have been delayed for some reason. There's
a party here tonight. Rao should be here in a while.
Please take off your coat and hat. It's raining outside,
isn't it? Your clothes must be soaked.'

'Oh, yes!' said the girl as she took off her coat and
hat. 'There's a light drizzle, and the fog's so thick
that it's suffocating.' And then, with a slight pause,
she said, 'Rao must have mentioned that I was to
come here this evening . . .'

Naim took the girl's warm clothing to the corner
and hung them on a peg. When he came back to the
fireplace, he saw that the girl was looking into the

mirror hanging on the cornice above the fireplace,
fixing her hair for a brief moment. After this, she
came close to the fireplace and stood near the flames
with her head lowered, and began to warm her hands.
She was wearing black clothes—a black woollen skirt
and a black coat of the same material. Underneath
the coat, she was wearing a deep-orange-coloured
sweater, a high-necked one that peeped out of her
coat. The fire was burning, and its rising flames
illuminated the girl's face.

Naimuddin liked the girl. The poor thing appears
to be well disposed, he thought, and sensible too. I'm
surprised that Rao never mentioned her to me. He
never told me that he had invited her tonight either.
But he's friends with so many women that it's
impossible to keep count! It seems she's a fresh catch.
Now, what should I tell her? If I say that Rao hasn't
mentioned her to me previously, the poor thing will
needlessly feel embarrassed; she'll think she's being a
burden on me. Rao is a strange man. If he had
invited her, he could have at least told me.

Naim felt peevish. What do I do now? Some
situation to be in! What do I say to her? Naimuddin's
tension was building up. What shall I do? What shall
I say? A storm of sorts erupted in his lazy mind.

The girl was standing quietly near the fireplace,
continuing to warm her hands. She did not even
remember that she had asked a question. There was
a sense of composure in her face. Rao will be here
soon. Perhaps I've arrived somewhat early, but it's a

good thing I did. How nicely the fire burns here, and this fat Indian student—he seems like a nice person too.

Meanwhile, Naimuddin continued to fret. Something had to be done. He headed towards the other corner of the room and, frowning to himself, took out a cigarette case from the pocket of his coat, which was hanging on a peg, and hurriedly approached the girl.

Breathing heavily, he said, 'Have a cigarette.'

The girl turned to face Naimuddin. 'Thank you very much,' she replied, and took a cigarette from the case. Naimuddin took one for himself and both lit their cigarettes. Naim relaxed a little. Good, the problem's been sorted.

'Please make yourself comfortable in this chair,' he said, trying to start a conversation.

'Thank you. I'm quite comfortable near the fire . . . but . . . very well then; I'll sit there. This chair is nearer the fire. But now I've stolen your chair. Where will you sit?' the girl asked with a laugh.

'Don't worry about me. I'll sit on this other chair,' Naim said, pulling a small armless chair in front of the bigger chair near the fire and sitting on it. Who is this girl after all? What does she do? Where could Rao have met her? She's an attractive one. Attractive. But *me*? Can anyone call *me* attractive? No girl falls in love with me. I wonder why . . . I'm very fat. Standing between me and love is a paunch. Who knows what this girl thinks of me? But what difference does a paunch make? Many of the world's great people had one. But if not the tummy, then what? Perhaps I don't have the knack to speak to women. Now this girl has been here for so long and I haven't been able to utter a single straightforward sentence. She must think how uninteresting and dull I am. But I've seen people who can't even utter two sensible words find love. So then what's the matter with me? My friends think that I'm not interested in such matters; that looking at a pleasant face doesn't have the least effect on me. Wrong. Absolutely wrong. *I have a pain in my heart; if I convey it, my tongue will burn.* I can't remember the other line right now. Is it true that my memory is gradually becoming weak? I've been wasting my time here for years. I haven't become dull, have I? The boy who used to sit next to me in school didn't understand anything and the poor thing would always fail in mathematics. I have never failed in my school and college examinations and have always passed with glory. Me, dull-headed? Says who? The number of poems by Mir and Ghalib that I've memorized ... perhaps no one else has. Anyone can make a bet with me. We'll see who wins. Can't I even utter a simple sentence right now? The poor thing's been sitting here for so long, and I haven't said a single word to her.

'Do you study law like Mr Rao?' the girl asked. She was half-lying on the chair. Cigarette smoke hung over her face and hair like a dim blue veil.

See! Tired of my silence, she's finally had to say something, Naim said to himself. 'No,' he replied.

'I'm a student of history. I'm attempting to earn a doctorate from the University of London.'

Attempting! I've used the word advisedly, thought Naim. The people who enrolled with me have long finished. Naim was on the verge of laughing aloud at himself but overcame the urge.

His eyes fell upon the girl's legs, which showed a few inches below her skirt. 'Are you a student too?' Naim asked the girl. Why didn't I ask this question earlier?

'Yes and no!' the girl responded with a laugh. 'Until last year, I was studying at University College; then I no longer had enough money to pay my fees, so I had to leave. Now I work at an office during the day and go to the college to listen to an evening lecture four times a week. I only have to pay a nominal fee.'

The answer pierced Naim's heart like an arrow. He who had no shortage of money, who had no worries about making a living, what did he do? How did he while away his time? His thesis showed no sign of getting completed. He was the target of his friends' jokes ... But it is one thing to write a thesis on an obscure treaty in Indian history and another to go in the evenings to listen to a lecture for an hour or two—which must enter through one ear and exit through the other. When my thesis is ready, it will be a valuable addition to historiography.

'On which subject do you hear lectures?'

'On art and philosophy,' the girl replied. 'Are you interested in them?' she asked.

Art and philosophy! Dear God. She appears to be an intelligent one. How shall I answer her question? Am I interested in art and philosophy? If I say yes, she'll begin to talk about the subjects, and I'm sure to say something stupid. What will she think then? Or is it possible that she has said this only to intimidate me? 'I am certainly interested,' replied Naim, 'but I've never studied these subjects in detail. It's for this reason, actually, that I can't say whether or not I understand art. And then there's philosophy, which requires a lifetime to become acquainted with. I'm surprised that you're interested in such dry subjects. Women are usually more interested in literature.'

'Please don't think that I'm well-acquainted with these subjects. I became hopelessly entranced studying literature in school and college. For two years I had such an interest in literature, especially poetry, that there was no limit. But there's been a strange change in me. The thought of poetry makes my hair stand on end. If you must know the truth, I understand nothing at all about philosophy. But listening to lectures and reading books on it gives me a kind of satisfaction— just as looking at a portrait done by a famous artist brings the heart comfort . . .' The girl's eyes, which were cast down, looked up at Naimuddin.

'But you must be thinking that I'm babbling a whole lot of nonsense,' she admitted with a sorrowful grin.

Naim was embarrassed. How could I have even thought that she intended to intimidate me with this kind of talk? Don't her face and eyes give witness to her truthfulness?

'No, no. Please don't think so. I'm listening to what you have to say with great interest. One very rarely gets the opportunity to speak with intelligent women here! And you must know that in India, men and women—especially young people—can't sit down like this and talk. Doing so is considered very improper ...' remarked Naim apologetically. 'But leaving all this aside, do tell me why you're no longer interested in literature, especially poetry? In my country, every educated person is absorbed in poetry and it's considered necessary to quote from poems in the middle of conversation, in speeches and in articles.'

'What! People quote poetry all the time in your country? What could be more frightful than that? If I lived in that sort of society, I'd go mad. The effect that poetry—good poetry—has on me is like moonlight on a pleasant summer evening. When we forget the light of the day and on everything—every disagreeable, unpleasant and meaningless thing—is cast a curtain: the sort of curtain that doesn't cover everything entirely, but hides only the defects, which otherwise hurt the eyes. This smokescreen casts itself over our hearts and minds, and sometimes causes our being to be immersed in a boundless ocean of pleasure and sometimes ... its pain knows no end.'

It appeared as though she was talking to herself. Her eyes were fixed upon the flames of the fire. The smile on her face faded. She sat up straight on the chair, paused for a moment and said, 'That's why I no longer enjoy poetry. I can't tolerate its effect.'

All of a sudden, Naim was gripped by the desire to find out about the girl's state of mind. He wanted her to continue speaking. Her voice was like the murmur of a flowing stream. Naim did not wish to interrupt her. He had no desire to hear his own voice. What's this girl saying? Her life must be overflowing with interests. Is she in love? Who knows what kind of love hers is! She must certainly be disappointed in her love; that's why she's talking like this. What sort of man would be her love?

But Naim felt repulsed by this thought. What's it to me? But even then her words are tinged with disappointment. This thought brought a little cheer to Naim. Why did she stop in the middle of the conversation? I should say something now . . . What shall I say? Her calves are really beautiful, and her toes too. She looks a little worried, though. She doesn't think me to be fat and uninteresting, does she? What should I say? This silence is painful. We were discussing poetry. Look at the flames in the fire, how they dance. I must appear clumsy while dancing because I'm fat. Why am I fat, after all? All this is the result of my laziness. It was a French poet, wasn't it, who declared 'Long live laziness. It is my beloved'? The line fits me perfectly. Is being fat a fatal imperfection? It's not that I'm *very* fat. I don't know what this girl thinks to herself when she looks at me. Who knows, maybe her thoughts never even

ventured in my direction. How absorbed she seems in
her thoughts. But now I should say something. How
improper dancing is considered in our country, the
trade of actresses and prostitutes. And if our maulvis
got a chance to watch a man and woman dancing,
their hearts would stop. Our poetry actually . . .

'It's possible that the reason for us Indians being
lazy is that we're immersed in poetry. You say that
the effect of poetry suspends our hearts and minds for
a little while, or that, at the very least, it takes them
away from reality and brings us to the world of
thoughts, and living in the world of thoughts, we
become so immersed that we begin to think that since
place and time are infinite, so are we. There's a
hidden desire for immortality in the heart of every
individual. We are able to quench this thirst through
poetry. Our mind says to us that some idea is stupid,
but using poetry we can even defeat our minds. Our
poetry is filled with the mind's sorrows. The mind
drags us towards hardship and pain. The mind can
trick us. But the wine of poetry! You yourself said
that it intoxicates us. And if this intoxication, this
state of ecstasy, this insensibility, drowns us sometimes
in the river of happiness and on other occasions in the
river of sadness in a way that we forget ourselves and
become a mere song of joy or a lamentation of loss,
we mustn't abstain from such a thing.'

Naim stopped suddenly: What's this I'm yammering
about without understanding? Hopefully this girl
won't think that the only reason I'm talking like her

is to prove my own philosophical knowledge. But Naim felt gratified. At least he was able to say *something*. The girl won't think that I'm completely ignorant. I'm actually *not* ignorant. I have quite a bit of sense in me; though it's true that I'm sometimes unable to give a meaningful response when the opportunity arises. This girl's lips are so nice; they're grape-like even without lipstick. What's her name? Why hasn't she told me her name yet? Her hair! If only I could touch it. My, my, the kind of irrelevant thoughts that are coming to me! A song of joy or a lamentation of loss. I am reminded of Zafar's poem:

> *I am not a life-giving melody, why should anyone listen to*
> *me;*
> *I am the voice of a great affliction; I am the complaint of*
> *a deep pain.*

And Ghalib:

> *Listen, O plunderer of human fidelity,*
> *Listen to the conquered heart's voice.*

And Mir:

> *An ache of sorts rises in the heart, a pain remains within*
> *the soul;*
> *I remain awake crying throughout the nights while the*
> *entire world sleeps.*

And Mir Anis:

> *Suddenly the tabla sounded, the clouds of the army bellowed,*
> *The mountain trembled, the ground shook and the jungle*
> *resounded.*

The beat of the tabla; a heart-rending sob; the melody of a song; the sound of a heart breaking. Why do I enjoy the cadence of this girl's voice?

'You're correct, but alas! We can't forget the bitter reality of life by humming songs,' replied the girl slowly.

'Maybe not forever, but surely for a little while? If the reality of life is bitter, it's better to forget it.'

'No, under no circumstances. Ignoring reality can never be better. Once your eyes open after the dream, this gilded dream, you'll find life to be darker, even more bitter, and more difficult.'

'This means that life, one's entire life, is a painful, intolerable, heavy burden, and we can never get deliverance from it! Quite a dreadful thought. How can you hold on to such a doctrine and remain alive?'

'I myself am astonished by this! Why am I alive? I'd ask this question of myself and feel scared answering it. I'd try to escape from it. The rhythm of life would lull me to sleep. The dreams that you've mentioned would render my soul senseless for a little while. But not for long. The riddle of my existence would remain unsolved. And like a boat without an anchor, without a sail, I'd be tossed about in the storm of life's sharp and piercing winds, left to fend off the crashing waves. This carefree existence was an oppressive, insurmountable burden. It was not life, but rather like being buried alive. It was death. As though we were breathing, the blood in our veins was flowing, but we were dead, our *souls* were dead.

There's nothing more dreadful than this. How
loathsome, how filthy, how ugly such walking corpses
are.'

She half-lay on the chair. Her eyes seemed to pierce
the black curtains of the room as they fell upon the
windows that were about a man's height.

An utter silence descended on the room. Only the
dry rustling of the fire and the distant noise of cars
moving on the road outside.

Am I a walking corpse too? Naim thought suddenly,
and his entire being shrivelled up and trembled, as
though he had accidentally touched an exposed wire.

'And what answer have you found for life's pressing
question?'

'I've heard it, felt it, have tried to understand it,
and am trying my best to give it meaning.'

'And in your estimation, after this exertion, this
mental and physical toil, the burden of life becomes
lighter?'

'The lessening of this burden shouldn't even be our
goal. Because it's impossible. But we can chisel this
precious stone, make it even more valuable, more
deserving of merit, and more beautiful.'

'The outcome of this effort? Its reward?'

'Life!' the girl said with fortitude. But her eyes
welled up with tears. She stood up and, pushing back
the black curtains, peered out of the window. The fog
spread out as usual, and on the road below, here and
there, lights flickered. And darkness all around the
circles of light.

4

Two more persons entered Naim's room—an Indian girl and a fellow she had brought along, both students.

'Come on in, Arif Sahib!' said Naimuddin. 'How are you? I'm very happy that both of you could come. We haven't got together for some time. I was afraid that my invitation wouldn't reach in time and that you wouldn't be able to make it.' Turning towards the girl, he said, 'Where are you these days, Karima Begum? I haven't seen you for two months. Please, both of you, take off your coats and come sit near the fire. I'll pull this couch nearer the fire. How terrible the weather is, and both of you live very far from here—one at Earls Court and the other at Golders Green. Where did you cross paths?' Naim continued to talk incessantly without waiting for his guests to reply and, at the same time, kept arranging the chairs in the room. Books, sheets of paper and newspapers were scattered everywhere. He cleared the couch and pulled it near the fire. An ashtray under his chair got kicked, and the ash spread all over the carpet.

The newcomers took two or three steps from the

door and then drew back in surprise. Their gaze had fallen upon the English girl standing between the black curtains near the window with her back to them, looking at the street outside. The duo glanced at each other. The dim lighting, Naim's anxiety, and his being alone with a girl: they put these pieces together in their minds and formed a complete picture; a significant grin formed on their lips.

'I'm sorry, perhaps we have arrived a little earlier than expected and caused you trouble,' said Arif.

'The fault's mine,' said Karima Begum with a jolt. 'I saw Arif Sahib at the students' association where I had gone to hear a lecture. It got over early and so I mentioned to Arif Sahib about my coming to your place. He said that he, too, was invited, and both of us took off without taking notice of the time.' She smilingly eyed the English girl who had now turned to acknowledge both of them. But Naim was still so lost that he paid no attention to his guests' gestures and winks.

'No, I think you've come at the right time. Why would your arrival cause me trouble?' asked Naim in a slightly worried tone.

The English girl now left her place near the curtains and moved towards the fireplace. Arif and Karima sat down as well, and all three of them gazed at each other. Naim took Arif's and Karima's coats and hung them on a peg in the corner.

Upon returning, he offered everyone a cigarette.

'No, thank you. I don't smoke,' said Karima in a faint, doll-like voice.

Naimuddin took a forceful puff of his cigarette. He was beginning to feel at ease. He felt like a tree which had trembled to its very roots in a hurricane and was now gradually returning to normalcy.

'I haven't introduced you. I'm very sorry. This is Mr Arif,' he said, bowing politely in Arif's direction, 'and this is Miss . . .' he stopped. He smiled at the English girl and said, 'I still don't know your name!'

The girl smiled. She shook Arif's hand and said, 'My name is Sheila. Sheila Green.' She turned towards Karima as well, and introduced herself.

'Would it be possible to have the light, Naim Sahib? It's hard to see anyone's face in this darkness,' remarked Arif, fixing the crease on his pants.

'Yes, yes, of course.' Saying this, Naim switched on the lamp hanging from the ceiling in the middle of the room. The place lit up.

Arif appeared to be a complete gentleman. His suit probably cost eight or ten guineas, and his demeanour revealed that he was aware of this. He smiled at Sheila so that the beautiful girl would pay attention to him.

'What do you think of this weather?' he asked her in his best attempt at an English accent.

Idiot! Naimuddin thought to himself. He doesn't know how to talk about anything other than the weather. Naim experienced an irritability of sorts; for some reason, Arif's smirk annoyed him. What does he think? He probably fancies himself very handsome. He thinks there's some kind of magic in his eyes that can turn any girl he likes into his slave.

'The weather? If you ask me the truth, I'd have to say that I don't think much about the subject,' answered Sheila as though roused from a dream. Then it seemed she felt she might have been harsh in her reply. She attempted to make amends.

'I was born in this weather; I've come of age in it. That's why today's bad weather doesn't have much of an effect on me. But you people, who are accustomed to the eastern sunshine, must curse our dark English weather.'

Arif was not expecting such a response and got the feeling that his first strike had been unsuccessful. He felt the need to think for a few moments. What should I say now, he asked himself.

'Dark weather! You're absolutely correct. Sometimes I have to turn on the lights in my room during the day as well.'

Karima Begum fixed the anchal of her rose-coloured sari and began chirping like a bird. 'Just think of it. I couldn't see anything in my room yesterday, at noon! And have you read the story in the newspapers? Someone snatched a young woman's bag from her hand. And this was near Hampstead, in broad daylight! The police couldn't make anything of it. I've heard that even murders occur there these days. Thieves and robbers attack lone women in the dark and scamper off after hiding their dead bodies under trees. I've heard that last year a girl's body was found in pieces there, except for her head, which was found six months later, packed in a box at the

Brighton station. And we used to think that the police here were clever. What intelligence did they show? There's still no trace of the murderer. I never go to Hampstead alone in the evening. Who knows—heh, heh, heh,' she chuckled dryly.

Naim began to worry again. What would Sheila think, listening to Karima? Chat, chat, chat, she keeps chattering—wretched, irrelevant nonsense.

'But, Miss Karima!' he said mischievously, 'the motive for attacking young women in Hampstead isn't always robbery.' Naim was certain that Karima would drop the subject. But he was disappointed.

'Then *what* could be the reason, pray?' Begum Sahiba queried with the innocence of a child.

Naim hesitated a little. Then, trying to be firm and to seem nonchalant, he replied in a deep voice: 'A man never endangers his life by attacking a woman for her riches and jewels. A woman's wealth isn't her money; it is her youth, her beauty; and for the hungry, thirsty male who puts his life on the line for these precious things—which in our society go to waste so often—the law can prepare its chains if it wishes, but under no circumstances should a liberal person point a finger of reproach in his direction. In my opinion, there should be respect in our hearts for the people who attack women in Hampstead.'

Karima Begum's face turned red with embarrassment and she lowered her eyes. It was as though some rascal had attacked her honour.

For all the unpleasantness of this inopportune and

impolite speech, it seemed that the greatest sense of its bitterness was felt by Arif.

He sensed that something had gone awry, and he began puffing on his cigarette, gazing at the ceiling.

Naim's glance fell upon Sheila, who was smiling. He was glad that Sheila understood that he was only saying these things in mischief.

'Naim Sahib, play the gramophone. Have you seen Maurice Chevalier's brand-new film? He sings a really great song in it. You must have his record. I bought a few records last week. One of them is his.' And then, turning towards Sheila, Arif asked, 'Do you like Maurice Chevalier?'

'I was quite interested in his films in the beginning. He had a freshness, a French charm, but his songs and films have nothing special in them now. In my opinion, the difference between a good and a bad artist is that one is never bored by a good artist. When you see him, it appears as though he's presenting us new spiritual gifts each time. The ordinary artist's treasury empties out quite early, and we often return empty handed from there. What do you think?' Sheila asked Arif.

Arif was somewhat confounded by this answer. 'What you say is absolutely correct. Maurice Chevalier isn't a first-rate actor. I've grown tired of him too. You're absolutely right. His treasury has now become empty.' And saying this, he laughed.

Flatterer! thought Naim to himself. He was complimenting Maurice Chevalier a moment ago and now he's criticizing him without thinking or understanding. And what's there to laugh about in all this?

But Sheila paid no attention to Arif's words. She asked him: 'What's the state of art in India? I'm certain that Indians, who are such attractive people, must be very good artists as well.'

Now Arif was at a loss for words. He had been so busy preparing for the Indian Civil Service exam, he hadn't found any time to pay attention to the fine arts. For two years, he had been occupied with preparing for the exam like the ox at an oil-press. He would study without break for eight to nine hours every day. Where could he have found time for intellectual refinement? It was the same in India. His family had decided, from when he was a child, that he would join the ICS when he grew up. It was whispered in his ear, day in and day out, that the ICS was his for the taking. Gradually, he and his relatives began to feel certain that he would pass the difficult exam, to think that it was their family's and Arif's birthright. What could be a more fitting career for the son of a noble Indian family than to be counted among India's rulers after reaching the glorious posts of magistrate and collector? After passing his BA, Arif had taken the ICS exam in India, but had been unsuccessful. In Arif's opinion and that of his family's, the reason for his lack of success was a Hindu examiner who had given him fewer marks because of his being a Muslim. Otherwise, how could it have been possible for someone like Arif to not pass the ICS exam! After Arif failed in India, his father decided that his prospects of clearing the exam were better in England. So he was sent to Europe. Here, too, he did his work conscientiously. It was very rarely that he would go to the cinema or theatre. Other Indian students would roam around aimlessly, chase girls, go to dancehalls, waste their time playing and jumping about, take part in politics. But Arif was the Majnoon of the Laila called the Civil Service. Like a mule, he continued working away on a straight path. Along with this, he took to wearing crisp English clothes, speaking English with a proper British accent, and keeping up with and speaking about motion pictures and the personal affairs of Hollywood actors and actresses—the fresh news of their weddings and divorces—as was the duty of an aspiring collector. He was about to become the successor of those who took pride in the fact that they did not know how to speak their mother tongue well, and who considered themselves to be even more 'authentic Englishmen' than the English themselves. There is a famous story about a 'Muslim' collector sahib belonging to the ranks of these people who asked his Muslim secretary on Bakra-Id: 'Well, Munshi! Is this a big day for *you* people?' That is how it was a generation ago; it is wrong to think that in the heirs of these 'authentic gentlemen', 'nobility' has given way to humanity.

'So, in your opinion, we Indians are attractive?' Arif turned around and asked Sheila, in an effort to evade a discussion concerning Indian art. He said 'we Indians' in a tone which gave the impression that he considered himself the keeper of all India's beauty.

Sheila responded, 'Yes, in my opinion, Indians are more attractive than the English, but it's possible that I'm incorrect in my assessment, because I've only seen a few Indians in Europe.'

Karima Begum, who had shrivelled up in the wake of Naim's rude words, tried to flap her wings again. 'Are you acquainted with many Indians in London?' she asked Sheila smilingly.

Boor! thought Naim. This woman doesn't say a thing that's appropriate! When she asks a question, she smiles as though flowers are being strewn when she speaks, but her heart is filled with poison! What business is it of hers how many Indians Sheila knows? The very thought of a man must cause a shiver to run through her body. Leave aside the fact that men pay her no heed.

'I'm not sure what you mean by "many",' replied Sheila. She paused for a moment, and then continued with a laugh: 'And there could be various meanings of "being acquainted", but right now we're discussing the physical appearance of Indians, for which "being acquainted" is not necessary.'

Excellent! thought Naim. An unmannerly question like that one deserves just such an acerbic reply.

Sheila continued, 'I'm very interested in India and everything that has to do with that country. One of my uncles was a civil servant there. I remember when he used to come back home during the holidays, he would bring back Indian toys for me. Dolls made of strange cloth, wearing colourful, shiny clothes, black hair made from thread, their long braids, their small faces and large dark eyes and eyelashes. I used to think India a fairyland, where handsome princes and beautiful dusky women, laden with gems and jewels, spent a life of sensual pleasure in large marble palaces. When I got older and began school and studied its history, my childhood ideas began to change. After reading about Sirajuddaulah and the terrible "Black Hole" story over and over again, and repeatedly hearing of the flaws of Indians and "black folks", a fear of sorts developed in my heart about every person belonging to a dark nation—in spite of the fact that my childhood interest in that distant, unknown country hadn't abated. When I enrolled in college, I made a special effort to meet Indian students, though my parents urged me to keep myself away from "dark people". Unfortunately, this special effort of mine had a very disappointing result. People began to have all sorts of misunderstandings about me. Thinking of these things now makes me laugh. The naive and stupid things I did!' Sheila fell quiet. There was a trace of a smile on her lips. She seemed to be ruminating about her past.

Karima Begum was beginning to feel anger towards the English girl. All this while Sheila was the centre of the entire discussion and everyone's attention.

Everything that Naim and Arif uttered was designed to please this wretched English girl. Arif had accompanied her from the club, but had forgotten her very existence when he saw the girl. Arif's becoming infatuated with Sheila, smiling at her, trying to get her to respond and repeatedly drawing her attention to his expensive suit and attractive physique through little gestures—these tactics were piercing Karima's heart like a thorn. She was surprised at Naim. Generally a silent, well-disposed, polite person, today he could not utter a *single* word properly. He was being sarcastic to everything Karima had to say and was treating her disrespectfully. He was furtively eyeing Sheila and smiling at her.

What's happened to these Indian men, for goodness' sake? They see fair skin and have no control over themselves. What does this European girl have besides her fair skin? How artificially she talks—making eye-contact with boldness! She wears tight-fitting clothes only so men can see her figure. Honourless. Shameless. Immodest. What's the difference between these women and prostitutes? Her hair is scattered like a witch's; there's powder on her face; her legs are sticking out from under her skirt; her socks are made of silk so sheer that it doesn't matter whether they are there or not. When she stands, she does so with haughtiness; and walks with a tense chest. She smokes cigarettes, drinks alcohol, dances—what attainments don't these Europeans have? Leave aside chastity and honour—which she carries around flippantly in the palm of her hand. If she snares a man today, she'll worry about trapping another tomorrow. There's no other purpose to such women's lives besides having fun, and Indian men fall into their trap once they come to Europe since they haven't a clue about the world around them. Where have they misplaced their sense, for heaven's sake? Someone tell me with what has this Sheila Green been blessed with that both of them seem to be ready to die for her? Some friend of Indians! She said she was always interested in India only to flatter these guys. Drunkard. Usurer. Christian. I know quite well what the reality of this friendship is! She said that Indians are very attractive, which was enough to turn these men on. And look at her cunning; how reluctant she is to answer my question! If she answered, she'd be exposed. Who knows how many Indians she's ruined! Deceit! It is as if these two have drawn a curtain across their reason. She doesn't seem educated. Flat-chested, pale-coloured, she comes off as a curse. Her body is like that of men—is she a woman or a wrestler? Nothing about her is gentlewomanly. She must be from a lowly family, the daughter of some pilfering worker. The English must not care for her. There are so many girls like her who are unable to find husbands here . . . All of them wandering about doing nothing. She is a woman of loose morals. She must be aiming to trap an innocent, rich Indian gentleman into marriage. She must hate us in her heart, but is ready to sell herself for wealth.

Karima Begum began to boil with rage. She felt like grabbing Sheila Green's hair with both hands, shoving her, and throwing her out of the room. At this point, she had assumed of her own volition the role of the sole defender of India's honour and dignity.

Arif, too, was beginning to feel disappointed with Sheila. He had repeatedly attempted to make an impression on the golden-haired daughter of fairies, but the girl paid no special attention to him. She is a strange one, he thought. I can't make her out. At times she talks about art, sometimes about the beauty of Indians. My presence makes no difference to her. She's arrogant; considers herself very able. She must certainly be a university student. The girls who make it to university begin to think of themselves as very learned.

But he refused to accept defeat. He who planned on ruling hundreds, thousands of people after passing the ICS exam, he whose one stern glance would make the hearts of poor Indians tremble (Arif was already getting drunk on the idea)—under no circumstance would *he* accept defeat at the hands of an ordinary English girl. She doesn't know who I am. Why, pray, did she mention the beauty of Indians? Arif remembered his entire record of stirring deeds. Was he not famous in India for being hardworking and intelligent? It's true that Hindu boys always beat him in exams. But that was because of the prejudice of Hindu professors. He always stood first among Muslims. And then Muslims don't tie their hair on the top of their heads and study all night long like Hindus. Governance is in their temperament. And to rule properly, it is not necessary for one to top the exams! Arif was upset that he was not selected for the ICS by virtue of his sincerity. It was his *right*, but another man was chosen instead of him because the other Muslim aspirant's family had a higher standing in the government's estimation. If he were in the ICS, Naim would have introduced him to Sheila as 'Mr Arif, ICS'. Oh well, if not now, then a year from now. He clenched his teeth and resolved to work an extra hour each day. And just as he would be successful in memorizing pages from books after hours of hard work, he decided that he would make an impression on Sheila Green.

Arif spoke up, 'Miss Green, I hope that you haven't allowed your bitter experiences to dampen your interest in India. There's no doubting the fact that Indian students who come to Europe often give proof of being uncivil. They don't have a clue about how to converse with and meet noblewomen here.'

Sheila began to laugh and then replied, 'My bitter experiences! Please be so kind as to not give these much importance. Such experiences are necessary for every inexperienced girl—without these, women don't understand. It was certainly not my intention to say that I find Indian students impolite. On the contrary, as I said, it was *my* fault. And for God's sake, please don't count me among noblewomen and ladies.' She glanced at Naim with great adulation and asked playfully: 'Am I actually so loathsome that you would think of me as a "noble"? I hope at least *you* don't think of me as being that dead and gone.' Then she got up and ran towards the mirror, stood in front of it and looked at herself from head to foot. 'No, no way! There's nothing to me that's like a noblewoman. What embellishment do I have on my face? Do my eyes lie? And my hands, take a look at my hands— do they look like the hands of a lazy, good-for-nothing? And when I speak, do I babble nonsense? Sometimes for sure, but not always. And my voice isn't the sort one would listen to and think that a bird is chirping. I'm unattractive for sure, *ugly* for sure, but at least I'm not a cheat, not a lie.' A childlike gravity came upon her face.

Naim roared heartily and, to cheer Sheila up, said, 'Miss Green, you can try however much you like, but a spot of nobility can never leave the skirt of your garment. It is inborn. God himself has placed the burden of nobility on your shoulders as a trust, and you wish to squander this precious treasure? That is impossible. Even attempting it would be useless.'

Sheila began to laugh too.

Arif did not know what to do. He suddenly became aware of his inadequacy. Why, after so many attempts, am I unable to utter a single word that the girl likes? And Naim is making a very good impression on her without saying much. He is neither attractive like me, nor is he well dressed. Why am I not successful? He immersed himself in these thoughts and, watching

Naim and Sheila laugh with such abandon, he too mustered a humiliated laugh.

Seeing Sheila laughing and conversing so, Karima Begum, like a skewered piece of meat, began to burn to a crisp.

5

A short while later, ten to fifteen people gathered in Naim's room—five or six women and eight or nine men. The gramophone began to play. People pushed the tables and chairs to the corners and began dancing. A group was sitting and talking; one of the invitees was holding a glass of alcohol, another was drinking lemonade or punch, a third was content with just a cigarette. Every few minutes, the music would stop after a record finished and the noise and clamour would subside a little. The dancers would break up; some would go to a seated group and join the discussion, others would remain standing and continue to chat, another would take a woman to a secluded corner and prattle amorously to her.

A couple of drunk men were speaking loudly. Azam was sitting alone, quiet, in a corner. Still no sign of Jean. The dancing, colour, noise, music and other people's laughter—everything was tormenting him. Depression had so overpowered him that he felt a stranger in this gathering—like a heavy rock in a flowing stream.

Rao, who had just finished dancing with Sheila, came up to Naim and stood there; Sheila followed. He was making fun of her.

'What's your opinion of this golden-haired Anglo-Saxon girl, Naim? She was alone with you long enough to have tried to inspire you with awe. And you, being the simpleton you are, would have fallen for it. But I understand this woman well. Philosophy, politics, India, the Vedas, Gandhi, Tagore—she's ready to venture an opinion on everything. I'm sure she must have got on *your* nerves too.'

'On the contrary,' replied Naim, 'making Miss Green's acquaintance and listening to her made me very happy. We were discussing life. Miss Green's thoughts on the matter are deeply interesting and worthy of consideration.'

Rao laughed heartily. 'Life! And a discussion about it! What could be a greater stupidity than that? How important, how magnificent an entity man fancies himself to be! But what is our status in the order of the universe? That of the most debased insects that crawl on the floor. And we give such importance to our life that it appears we're the centre of the universe! How ludicrous!'

Karima Begum, too, was sitting to one side and talking.

'But Begum Sahiba,' said the man who was conversing with her, 'your efforts are in vain. You say that we should only learn virtues from Europe, not the vices; and you propose to us the sort of ideal in which Indians, leaving aside all their vices, combine their virtues with those of Europeans and become the world's best creation! There can be two objections to this proposal. The first is that the virtues and vices of a society aren't given currency because of an individual's personal opinions and liking. You find many defects in Europe. For instance, you say that the measure of freedom given to women here is leading them along a destructive path. What we need to see is, why these customs and practices came into existence, why new measures were implemented in European life. Five hundred years ago, the status of women here was about the same as that of today's Indian woman. But in the ensuing period, a powerful revolution took place in Europe's economic system, the effect of which was also felt on the social and political order here—the reason why a revolution was brought about in the European mentality. The customs and practices here changed. The European of today is the product of all these changes. The roots of his virtues and vices run back to his social order. A great many fundamental changes are taking place in India as well—which you, more than necessary, consider to be happening under the influence of Europe—and it's because of these changes that it's progressing. There are virtues in these and vices as well. To merely look at them and not glance at their root is folly. And the second objection . . .'

A couple of men and women came to stand around both of them. Someone cut into the discussion and asserted, 'My second objection to Mr Ahsan is that he doesn't have any right to give a speech here. We've come here for a party, not to hear a lecture. This is why I propose that Ahsan and Karima Begum stand up at once and dance with each other.'

Karima Begum was somewhat calmed now that she found herself the centre of the crowd's attention. Three or four men began to insist that she dance with Ahsan. Ahsan laughed as well, and stood up.

'Certainly, I'm ready.' And bowing before Karima Begum, he said, 'Will you give me the honour of this dance?'

Karima Begum smiled; she adjusted the anchal of her sari and, turning her head, said, 'I'm helpless; I don't know how to dance at all.' Then she was suddenly reminded of how shameless a thing dancing is and felt angry with Indian—especially Muslim—men who had forgotten their customs to such an extent in this foreign land that they didn't even have the least bit of shame in entertaining the thought of an Indian Muslim girl dancing. She said to Ahsan in a sarcastic tone, 'It appears that you've forgotten that dancing is considered *improper* where we come from.'

In the meantime, the music began to play again. People resumed dancing. But Ahsan sat next to Karima Begum.

He thought to himself: Has this girl come to these conclusions after considering these matters seriously, or is she talking out of a narrow-minded conservatism? People who come from India often express such thoughts in the beginning. I, too, was opposed to dancing two years ago. But now . . . His thoughts got scattered in the noise and clamour. He said to Karima Begum, 'No, I certainly haven't forgotten that dancing is considered a vice where we come from, but I wish only to ask you one question and it is this: What's the measure of virtue and vice? Who decides that this custom is good and that one bad? This is the second objection I have. You travelled alone from India to this very distant land of disbelievers; you don't observe purdah; you're proficient in the English language; you're gracefully adorned in a sari, which is the attire of Hindus; you're present at a gathering of males who are not related to you; you're speaking to me with enthusiasm: are these things not considered improper where we come from?'

'When did I say that everything about us is good and everything to do with Europe is bad? All I'm against is the blind imitation of things here,' replied Karima Begum.

'And I'm against the blind imitation of anything, not just Europe,' said Ahsan, raising his voice. 'For hundreds of years in India, women would perform sati because that was their religious obligation. For hundreds of years, around the world, weaker individuals were enslaved; the slave trade flourished in almost every nation, and no one uttered a word against it. But today these things are considered the darkest attitudes ever nurtured by humanity. The things that were thought of as acceptable yesterday are considered shocking today. Why? That's not all; you'll also find that regarding each of life's major problems, there exists a strong difference of opinion among people of different classes. For instance, these days a group believes that those who don't give back to society by putting their mental and physical powers to use are like ugly and poisonous blisters on the body of the nation, which ought to be cut out and thrown away. On the other hand, another group thinks wealth and influence to be its rightful inheritance and shamelessly considers the fruit of others' labour its birthright. Who's wrong and who's right? Who's truthful and who a liar? How might one decide this?'

This fellow worries me, Karima Begum began thinking. What did I say that made him come after me with a stick? He sure knows how to talk. Even so, her hatred towards those Indian students who came to Europe to study—and, having arrived, wasted their time merrily dancing about—did not abate. Is this why our parents sent us seven thousand miles away? The reason, perhaps, why my parents were against my going to Europe to study. But I came here through my own effort, winning a scholarship. I'm not like these people who squander their parents' savings and who, once they scrape through their exams, return home after years. And the icing on the cake is that they often take back a memsahib with them! Why did I come here today? I was certainly in the right to have stopped meeting Indians in London altogether. This Ahsan Sahib who's arguing with such gusto, he's hardly an angel. That day when you were eating with an Englishwoman at Shafi restaurant, you turned your face away, pretending not to recognize me. But on your way out, you had to pass by my table and were forced to greet me. For my part, I snapped back in such a way that you probably still can't forget.

'I don't know about all this,' replied Karima Begum peevishly. 'But I don't see the good in dancing, drinking and chasing English women.'

'And when did I say that I wish to see these antics become the aim and purpose of the lives of Indian students?' There was anger in Ahsan's voice.

A voice came from one side, slurred due to alcohol. 'London . . . L . . . London, I hate this sh . . . shity. There'sh nothing here that'sh likeable. Likeable . . . I . . . I shay. Do you know w . . . what happened today? I went to Regent Palash thish after . . . noon. The plan wash to catch a girl. A girl—'

'Oh, Khan, old chap, don't speak so loudly. There are women here as well. What'll they say if they hear you?' someone petitioned.

'To hell with women. What'sh it to . . . what'll they ru . . . ru . . . ruin of mine? Lishen to my shtory! T . . . two women were sheated near me. One was sort of an old hag, but the other w . . . one was kind of delishioush, young—over and over again, she'd look my . . . way. I caught on at onsh that she wanted to shpeak to me. But I thought to myshelf that the young one'sh fine, but how to get rid of the old wr . . . wr . . . wretch!'

'How old was she? Now she couldn't have been that old. You should have brought both of them along, my friend; someone else would have benefited,' a man cut in.

'Don't interrupt,' said Khan, becoming irritable. 'I began to ogle the y . . . young girl, too, then she shmiled at me—'

'Why do you lie, old chap? Try your tricks on someone else. You used to have luck with the best of them. But when you went to Regent Palace with me today, not a single woman even glanced at you; smiling's out of the question. You're not so handsome that women go weak in the knees as soon as they set their eyes on you.'

'Shingh! Don't in . . . terrupt, I tell you. Or elsh it w . . . w . . . won't be good,' said Khan Sahib querulously.

'Oh, well, you're handsome all right. Do tell us what happened,' retorted Singh with a chuckle.

'Then I began talking . . . to her. This is shumthing that takesh a great deal of courage. If Shingh wash in my plash, he'd find that not even a sh . . . sh . . . shingle word would eshcape hish lip . . . s. Do you know how I shtarted the dishcushion?'

'I know,' said Singh. 'You would have pulled out your golden cigarette case from the pocket of your waistcoat with great pride and offered those poor women Abdullah cigarettes.'

'Wr ... wr ... wrong, completely wrong!' said Khan, moving his head up and down. 'When my glansh fell upon the young girl'sh f ... f ... fingersh, I s ... saw that s ... she wash wearing a ring. I immediately shaid, "How fine an emerald thish ish! If I ... it'sh not any trouble, pleash allow me to have a look at thish p ... precioush jewel for a s ... s ... second. We Oriental ... s are big enthu ... shiasht ... s of thesh thingsh." That wash it; that wash en ... nough. She under ... shtood that I'm not shum bankrupt shtudent, but a n ... n ... nobleman who has great knowledge about jewelsh. Hear me, Shingh ... Shahib, I'm a nobleman. I didn't come to Europe sho I'd bushy mysh ... elf worrying day and night about pashing examsh like s ... s ... schoolboysh. I can shtay here for however many daysh ash I wish, and I can leave whenever I w ... w ... wish.'

Rao, too, was hearing Khan Sahib talk. 'Why are you being so ceremonious? Say it clearly that you're a prince, a shahzada. The smallest of small Indian landlords come to think of themselves as shahzadas once they come to Europe and add "prince" before their names to impress the gullible women here.'

'Doesh shumone doubt my nobility?' said Khan Sahib looking here and there. 'I'm a nobleman, my father ...'sh a nobleman, my great grandfather wash a nobleman—we've been leader ... s for generation ... s. King Akbar gave my ansheshtor the title of panch hazari, commander of five thoushand troopsh.

He went s . . . shtraight from Bokhara to Delhi, and arriving there, held a very high rank in Akbar's c . . . court.'

'So what makes this something to be so proud of? He might have cleaned the droppings of Akbar's horses, for all we know. If you want to see lineage, look at mine! I'm a Chandarbansi Rajput—a descendant of the moon. We never lowered our heads in front of the enemy,' declared Singh.

'And now the decendants of panch hazari chiefs and the brave Rajputs *both* lick the tip of the boots of the English with great pride,' said Rao.

'And what do y . . . *you* do?' Khan and Singh chimed in together, combative.

'I'm studying law in order to take advantage of the stupidity of you men of breeding,' answered Rao laughingly.

'All of you—noblemen, shopkeepers, moneylenders, barristers, lawyers, doctors, professors, engineers and government servants—are like leeches who thrive on the blood of India's workers and peasants. This condition won't last until the end of time. One day, the thousands, *millions* of miserable people in India will wake from their sleep. On that very day, all of you will be finished forever,' said Ahsan in his heavy Punjabi drawl.

'Where did thish Bolshevik come f . . . from?' retorted Khan Sahib peevishly.

'Ahsan Sahib, what do *you* do that you criticize others like this? The twenty pounds you receive from home every month don't drop from the sky into your father's hands! As far as I know, he, too, is a government officer; the salary he receives is, according to your own words, the blood of Indian workers and peasants. What service are *you* performing for India's poor here? Like other Indian students, you'll also try to find a job after getting your degree. What's the point of criticizing us, then?' said Singh with a sarcastic grin.

Before Ahsan could muster a response, Rao spoke up.

'I agree with Ahsan. We are no better than thieves and robbers. Who can say that we have a right to India's wealth, which we're squandering here? Of what benefit is our life to India? None! But I say that as long as there are such fools present in this world, who give unworthies like us the opportunity to cheat them in broad daylight, as long as India's people who work for their wages enjoy being kicked around, it's an absolute waste of time to worry one's head over that herd of sheep and strive for its betterment. We, who are fortunate and who have a fair bit of plundered and ravaged wealth in our possession, should try to have a swell time without worrying. God knows what might happen tomorrow!'

'Oh, f . . . friendsh!' shouted Khan Sahib, 'shtop thish talk of po . . . po . . . politicsh. Wherever one goesh, th . . . ish wretched politicsh chashesh after one'sh tail. It'sh become difficult to shteer clear of it. Shum k . . . character . . . s thesh people are, acting like Bolsheviksh! India has nothing to do with Bolshevishum. I've heard that wo ... wo ... women have become national property in Russia—whoever wish ... esh can take any girl and ...'

Ahsan, who was standing, turned towards Khan Sahib placed a hand on his shoulder, and whispered softly: 'Is this all you've heard about Russia? Listen to another piece of news; I'll give it to you. Before the revolution, animals like you lived in Russia. The Bolsheviks turned them into fertilizer for their land.'

When the six-foot-tall, burly Punjabi youth placed his hand on poor Khan Sahib's shoulder and spoke the way he did, all of Khan Sahib's intoxication fled in a fit of terror. He was a fragile, thin scion of a noble family. Left trying to skulk in his chair and giggling in a bid to cover up his humiliation, he said, 'You've become angry, my friend! I was just joking. What do *I* know about Russia? I was just repeating what I've heard.'

Without answering, Ahsan turned away and addressed someone else.

'Hello, everybody!' a newly arrived girl said in a loud voice. People were dancing. A couple of men answered her greeting and got back to the dance.

But Azam's heart began to pound; this was Jean's voice. She had decided to come after all! But how distressful, how unbearable a wait it was. And when he heard her voice, the distress turned into anguish. While waiting, his condition had been like that of a taut bow-string, impossible to stretch further. And now his emotions had become tremulous, as though, upon reaching the limit, they had been released—like an arrow from a stretched bow.

Azam did not rise from his seat. He could not make up his mind as to how he would greet Jean. But her eyes found him after looking all about. She hurried to him, and taking his face in her hands, lifted it towards her. Azam remained silent; not a single word could escape his lips. He sensed that Jean's presence was gradually making his heart feel less constricted. But this was only in the outer reaches of his heart. Jealousy furiously agitated the core. The light of love in the dark purgatory of his heart, like a lamp's flickering flame, became weak, close to being snuffed out.

'Please, please, don't be so cross with me,' said Jean with a smile. 'Will you stop talking to me altogether? I tried very hard to come on time, but what could I do? I wasn't able. The fault isn't mine.'

Is it *mine*, then? Azam thought to himself. He spoke out loud: 'Jean, you're three hours late. I waited for you at Russell Square for close to an hour. If you'd told me earlier that you wouldn't be able to make it, I wouldn't have had to wait.' He was astonished that he had spoken to her in so gentle a tone.

Jean removed her hands from Azam's cheeks and, like a penitent child, stood up hanging her head; she would look occasionally at Azam through side glances. She made a face and said, 'But, darling, I wanted to come earlier. I got caught up with work at the last moment. What could I do? I had to iron my clothes; after that ... after that my brother's friends came over and dragged me to the cinema with them. I made a thousand excuses, but they didn't accept even one. It was a very good film and today was the last screening. If I hadn't gone now, I'd never have had the chance to watch it.'

'Going to the cinema and ironing clothes are so important in your opinion that three hours of my day could be wasted! Don't you feel ashamed saying that? You could at least lie and say you had something *important*,' yelled Azam. He was feeling a strange, gloomy happiness about the fact that his heart's voice had reached his lips. He had never spoken to Jean in a fit of anger. All the same, he was conscious of an intense misery immediately after. Is this the same girl I was smitten with, after seeing her for the first time two years ago? How these two years have passed: happiness at times, grief and worry at others. And now we have reached a stage where I'm speaking to her in anger and her words are tormenting me. This is my beloved, the girl I'm in love with. Love? Passion? Have I been fooling myself for so long? A dreadful thought.

Meanwhile, Khan Sahib's voice reached Azam's ears. 'Who's this lass, my friend? The one that's talking to Azam? She looks dazzling. I like her a lot ...'

'I've told you many times not to yell so loudly. That's Azam's sweetheart. If he hears what you're saying, he'll break your head,' warned Singh.

Khan Sahib's lack of good manners angered Azam. His thoughts were diverted. Jean placed her hands around his neck and sat on his lap. Then she said slowly, 'Forgive me', and before Azam could offer a response, kissed his lips.

At that very moment, Rao passed by and, laughing, he protested, 'Hey! You can't do that here.'

Jean immediately got up from Azam's lap. After shaking hands with her, Rao said, 'Well, you left us standing at Russell Square for an hour!'

'I'm very sorry, Mr Rao. Do something about Azam for me. He's so angry with me that he won't even talk.'

'Oh, Azam!' said Rao. 'Don't be an idiot. Whatever happened, happened. Stand up and dance with Jean.'

'Yes, come,' said Jean and, taking Azam's hand, pulled him out of the chair.

The gramophone was playing a song:

Love brings us to life,
Love saves us,
Love makes us happy,
Love makes us sad,
Love! Strange love!

Jean and Azam began to dance.

Arif was anxious to go home. His evening had been wasted. The entire evening! Just think how much work could have been done in this time. All sorts of awkward questions are asked in the oral exam, so it is necessary to keep up with the newspapers. That was why Arif read the *Times* every day like a prayer and occasionally copied out good sentences from it on a separate sheet. After this, he would try to commit them to memory. While chatting with friends, he would often steer the conversation around to topics on which he could use these sentences. He hoped that in this way, not only would his acquaintance with the English language improve, but the opinions of the *Times* would become firmly entrenched in his mind. This newspaper's point of view is the point of view of England's 'great gentlemen'. Whatever is published in the *Times* is thought of as 'semi-official'.

Arif wished to become completely immersed in governmental thinking and hoped that, when the time for the exam came, not a single word to which the imperialist examiners would have the slightest objection would escape from his pen or mouth. In continuing to adopt as his own the opinions of others, his brain had become like a gramophone, but he lacked any consciousness of this. It had become such a habit for him to deal in fake coins that he had begun to fancy them real. And why wouldn't he think this way? Day and night, his family would say its prayers pleading that, somehow, he be successful in the ICS exam. University students in India would often go for a government job. Most of his friends kept themselves busy preparing for one exam or the other. In England, too, most Indian students could be counted as belonging to this group. The few that remained outside that circle, Arif would always keep his distance from.

Of these sorts of people, it was only Naimuddin whom Arif visited every two or three months; and that, too, because Naim was a distant relative. Apart from this, he would occasionally go to the Indian students' union to eat Indian curry and rice. But he always took great care to sit at a table with students who, like him, were preparing for some government exam.

He remembered an incident when, because of lack of space, he found himself having to eat with Ahsan and Rao. Ahsan had proceeded to ask him tough, unusual questions, and because of his taunts and reproaches, had made it difficult for Arif to eat in peace. Ahsan had wondered out loud, 'Arif Sahib, if you're made a magistrate in a district and we start a political disturbance there, will you send us to jail? Will you give the order to open fire on our marches?'

He had worriedly answered, 'Duty is duty. But why do you assume that I'll imprison innocent people and open fire on those who haven't committed a crime?'

At this, Ahsan laughed heartily and replied, 'Then say that you've already conceded that a foreign English government's duty is your duty and that you're totally willing to execute it!'

'What else *should* he do?' asked Rao, joining in. 'The benefits of executing the master's orders are apparent. Wealth, power and a fair bit of authority over poor natives. There isn't an atom's weight of gain in joining hands with crazy people like you. Rather, it's the opposite: there's nothing but ruin.

First of all, no one pays attention—you can yell "freedom" a thousand times. If you scream a lot, throw a tantrum, you breathe the air of the jailhouse; your wife and children die hungry. It goes without saying that when you're released after a couple of years, your health is splendid after eating bread mixed with dirt for so long. And so after that there's only one path remaining! That of worship. Sit at home and remember God. And after a few days, depart to the other world. When the other path leads you to this destination, what wrong has Arif committed if he's latched on to the English one?'

'Right. Right! Absolutely right,' replied Ahsan. 'It was Akbar, wasn't it, who said, "Eat bread, do clerkship, swell up with happiness"? The only problem is that one can't even find bread and a clerkship now. That's why many among us "noble" youngsters are forced to join the battalion of the hungry.'

The discussion had continued in the same vein. Finally, Arif rose after eating hurriedly. It was after much praying that he received deliverance from these freethinking students. In his heart, he bore a hatred of sorts for such types.

They're envious of us, he thought. If they got the same jobs they're making fun of, they'd gladly accept them and would abandon nationalism and Bolshevism forever. In reality, these people run away from hard work! They know that they'll never be able to pass a difficult exam, and so they sit in London, spout politics and enthusiastically curse the government.

All their bragging disappears once they return to India. Every morning, they arrive at the bungalow of the magistrate they make fun of here, greet him, and even listen to his orderly's rebukes.

Arif saw that Rao and Ahsan were sitting in a corner, talking. He was glad that the two were not seated near him. Arif did not wish to be trapped in such circles. He quietly got up from his place and set his eyes on the girls in the room. He had a sudden urge to meet some girl, dance with her, and be gratified by her company. The defeat he had just suffered was still lingering in his heart. He decided that if no girl agreed to leave the party with him, he would pick up some whore strolling in the lanes near Piccadilly.

The room was filled with cigarette smoke. The light was not too bright either. Embers were glowing in the fireplace. The flames had died down. Behind the black curtains, it appeared as though a man and a woman were kissing. The girl's muffled laughter, the scream of music, conversation, a burst of laughter, the continuous twirling of dancing pairs—all these were stirring Arif's feelings.

He approached a dark-haired, plump girl, and asked, 'Will you join me for a dance?'

The girl turned towards Arif and replied cheerfully: 'Of course!'

Arif began to dance with her. He was not concerned about the girl. All he sensed at that moment was that a soft and delicate body was sending waves of heat to his heart and mind.

Rao was talking to Naimuddin after taking him aside.

'Oh, Naim! What's come over you? I've never seen you enamoured of anyone before. But today you haven't stopped pursuing Sheila; you've been hovering around her. At the least, you should consider that *I* invited her here and that she's *my* friend! Either you don't even glance at a girl or, if inclined towards one, you don't care that you are seducing a friend's!'

Naim chuckled. 'You have dozens of female friends; if you lose one, you won't even notice it. But tell me the truth: Are you genuinely interested in Sheila?'

Before Rao could answer, Sheila spoke up: 'What's this that you two are plotting against me?' Sheila's laughing voice came from a distance. She had probably heard her name in their conversation. She rose from her place and stood between Rao and Naim.

'Plotting against you! Who can speak ill of you?' said Rao. 'Right now, the discussion was regarding whether or not one can fall in love with you!'

Naim's face turned red. He was somewhat angry with Rao. What an idiot Sheila would take me for!

'How interesting,' remarked Sheila, grinning. 'And what conclusion did you arrive at?'

'The one that I've always stood by—that you place an undue importance on love. There's nothing in it other than sex, and whatever else people say about love, it's all the drapes of poetry to hide the reality. Since we Indians are more spiritual compared to you savages of the West, we understand the reality of everything better than you do, and can arrive at the

path of truth more easily than you. That's why, after
having arrived at the root of mutual relations between
men and women, our society has firmly protected it.
We have removed love and passion from our homes—
thrown them out like trash. In the same way that
pigeons are paired by being closed in dovecotes, our
men and women are locked up in a small room after
much pomp and celebration. We call this ritual a
"wedding". Certainly, some jester must have chosen
that name. Miss Sheila Green, you've met many
Indians, but it appears that our spiritual civilization
has had absolutely no effect on you.'

Sheila began to laugh. Naim was smiling as well.
He felt it was a good thing Rao was speaking to
Sheila like this. Although Naim himself couldn't speak
to a girl so openly, he felt that his participation in the
discussion would make it easier for him to be informal
with Sheila. Now he was certain that she wasn't one
of those politer-than-necessary women with whom
one dreads speaking candidly, out of fear that they
would consider the discussion of sensitive topics
unmannerly.

He wondered what the reason behind Rao's casual
manner could be. Is he in love with Sheila? No, if
that were the case, he would have mentioned it to
me. Maybe the two went to college together and
became friends.

Sheila said lightly, 'And how great a specimen you
are of this spiritual civilization! I'd certainly have
fallen prey to your spirituality if it weren't for your

remarkably good looks. I don't fancy being locked up with you in a small room; looking at you, one wishes to prostrate on the ground like a worshipper.'

Rao began to chuckle as well. 'Now I'll commit suicide,' he said. 'What I say has no effect on you. Every time I try to declare my love for you, you put me off by bringing out some new objection, some new excuse, some new argument. Eastern spirituality, the West's materialism, my good looks, our youth—you don't care about a single thing. Sheila Green, the cup of my patience has overflown. I'm leaving. Goodbye.' He bowed to Sheila, turned around, and went to the other part of the room, bracing himself as if he were a soldier preparing to be martyred. There, he began to joke around with the other guests. Sheila and Naim were left standing alone.

'I like Rao,' Sheila said to Naim. 'I've known him for a number of years, but I've never found any change in his character. Talking to him, it seems he doesn't have a favourable opinion about anything in the world, especially things that ordinary people look to with respect. Someone who doesn't know Rao well would think him quite heartless, that he has no affection, no respect for anything. But this isn't actually the case.'

'He's a dear friend of mine as well,' said Naim, 'and of all the people I know, he's the brightest. But sometimes I fear his intelligence will go to waste. It isn't enough for us to pass exams and be able to engage in delightful conversation. Whenever I think about what Rao will do once he gets back to India, I am unable to come up with an answer. I don't have this worry about most Indian students—their being and not being in this world doesn't matter. But Rao who, because of his intelligence, can understand everything at once, can get to the bottom of everything within a minute—if he too gets lost in this group, I'll feel sad.'

'Yes, you're quite right, Naim. Indian students go over the top in their speechifying; so much so that they connect the earth with the sky. There isn't another group more talkative than Indian students. They discuss minor points for hours, leaving the real subject aside. When they joke around, they tear each other apart. And they yell so much, it seems as though a fight is about to break out among them. Whenever I meet Indian students, I wonder deep down whether the lives of these people, who love and yearn to talk so much and who have such allurement in their eyes, are also filled with such passion . . .' She paused. Naim did not say anything. After a brief silence, Sheila continued in a low voice, 'At least I know one Indian about whom the answer to this question can be given in the affirmative.'

Naim blurted out, 'Who? What's his name?'

'You wouldn't know him. I met him a number of years ago in Switzerland.' Then, looking about, she queried, 'Don't you dance, Naim? I've been here at your place for so long and you haven't asked me to dance even once. Amazing! Some host you are!'

Naim understood that Sheila wanted to change the subject. She was smiling, but there was the shadow of sorrow in her eyes. It seemed as if she was being held captive in that room; everything and everyone seemed to have become a burden to her at that moment. Sheila herself felt that her voice had turned hollow, colourless. She looked at Naim in a way that made it clear that, without saying it in so many words, she was seeking his help, his sympathy. Why? Why? Naim asked himself, and the question shot through his heart and mind like a bullet.

'I don't dance well,' said Naim. 'You wouldn't enjoy dancing with me. But if you don't care about your feet getting crushed, I'll happily dance with you.'

'If I had that fear, I wouldn't know how to dance to this day,' Sheila replied with a laugh.

Sheila and Naim began dancing. Their feet were moving to the rhythm of the music, but there was a degree of slowness to them, a heaviness of sorts.

Naim's mouth and nose would sometimes brush against Sheila's hair. Her right hand was in Naim's left. He could feel that Sheila's hand was cold as ice. He held it firmly and his heart began to beat furiously. In that moment of ecstasy, sometimes a dim thought would enter his heart and mind, and disappear.

The pleasure of being close to this girl has struck me like lightning; how long will it last?

Naim, Naim. Have you fallen in love with this girl?

Why do you insult the name of love! Do you know what love is? An ecstasy is casting its spell over you.

Naim, your heart was made for love—the same way that a honeycomb is made for honey.

Aren't you ashamed of lying? Wretch! Don't you know you're not worthy of this?

What should I do, for God's sake! Tell me. Is one not permitted to quench his thirst in this Karbala?

It is not just that you are thirsty. Your heart is of no use because it's worthless. You're even worse than those travellers who fell down, weary, along the way, or those who are prepared to go back. You haven't even begun walking.

Ah! But her lips! Their sweetness, their softness, the feverish moistness; her eyelashes, which flash again and again in silence; and the delicate, intense, sparkling pupils in her big eyes that prance around here and there! Her entire body. These are all mine, they ought to be mine.

Has anything to this day ever been given for free? What do you have?

In that case, is there no hope for my escape? Have the doors of happiness closed on me forever?

As long as the dance continued, a complete silence cast itself over Sheila and Naim, and when the music stopped all of a sudden, the dancing couple appeared as though roused from a dream. They stopped like the others, holding each other's hands, and moved towards a corner of the room. Once there, Naim said softly, in a voice so faint that it was difficult to hear, one word, 'Sheila', and kissed her hands.

Sheila, too, whispered 'Naim' very softly, and pressing his hand a bit, let go of it.

6

(I)

It must have been around one o'clock in the morning when there was a knock at Naimuddin's door and a woman came in. Everyone's eyes turned towards her. It was the landlady, an old woman. She was thin and tall, her hair white; she was wearing black.

'Mr Naim,' she said, after looking about, 'I'd like to speak to you alone for a minute.'

Naim stopped the music; the noise in the room subsided as well. A peevishness and anger appeared on everyone's face as a result of the interruption of their sensual pleasure.

As the host, Naim sensed this unpleasantness and spoke up. 'Everyone continue talking and dancing. I'll be back shortly.' Then he proceeded towards the door, where his landlady was standing.

'Who's this aunt of Shaitan? Why has . . . shh . . . e b . . . b . . . barged in here?' yelled Khan Sahib.

'Don't yell, Khan; it's the landlady. If she throws you out of the house, all your bluster will disappear,'

Singh admonished. But Khan Sahib had drunk so much that he was not in his senses.

'No b . . . bugger can throw me out of here,' he asserted, nodding his head and cursing in English.

In the meantime, someone turned on the lights; the landlady glanced at the entire group, her nose in the air. Someone was lying on the floor, snoring; someone else was sitting near the fire, his hand on his sweetheart's back; yet another was standing hidden behind the curtains; people were scattered about any which way. The old woman glared at Khan Sahib, suddenly opened the door and stormed out. Naim left with her.

'And so, that's as far as your bravado goes, does it? The old woman glanced at you once, and you were struck dumb,' Singh teased Khan.

Khan Sahib stood up in anger and, staggering, came to the centre of the room. After swaggering back and forth and waving his hands all about, he replied, 'Shingh Shahib shuggesht . . . s that I fell sh . . . shilent out of fear. Thish ish falsh, completely falsh. No one can f . . . forsh me to shtop talking. I challenge everyone in this gathering. I'll begin talking, shtanding here. Shumone shit down with a watch and note down for how long I continue. If any gentleman here talksh l . . . l . . . longer than me, I'll give him a pound. If I win, he will have to give me the shame amount.'

Everyone in the room began laughing. They forgot about the landlady and began clapping.

Trying to make himself heard above the commotion, Rao spoke out aloud, 'Is there someone willing to accept Khan Sahib's challenge? Singh, you keep teasing Khan; now it's your duty to accept his challenge.'

'Fine,' replied Singh, 'provided that Khan Sahib begins talking first and doesn't stop till he gets tired.'

'That's absolutely right. Your challenge has been accepted, Khan Sahib. Begin. It's twelve minutes and thirty seconds past one right now. Are you ready? One ... two ... three ... start!' Rao stood near Khan Sahib with a watch.

People gathered and formed a circle around Khan.

'One was pretty good, the other, a w ... w ... worthlesh old woman ...' Khan Sahib began his account.

'Oh, golly, you've already told this story. Tell us something new,' someone remarked.

It appeared as though Khan Sahib did not hear him. He continued, 'It wash out of compulsion, a shtrong compulsion that I had to feed b ... b ... both of them in the end. I thought that now I'd at leasht be able to d ... do away with that old hag. But, f ... friendsh, she showed no shi ... gnsh of b ... budging. It became dif ... ficult to talk to the other one. I shaid to myshelf—'

'At which restaurant did you feed them?' asked Singh, in a whisper audible to all.

Khan Sahib stopped mid-sentence. He suddenly turned towards Singh in anger and yelled, 'To hell with the ch . . . ch . . . challenge. By God, if I ever shpeak to you again, I'm not the shon of a Pathan but a shoemaker'sh b . . . b . . . bashtard child! Do you think I don't have money to feed two girlsh that you ashk shuch k . . . question . . . s! Shum pershun *you* are to be ashking thish! "At which r . . . r . . . reshtaurant did you feed them?" What'sh . . . it to you?'

'There's no need to get angry, Khan Sahib. You're a nobleman, all right. What's one pound, ten pounds— it's nothing to you. If you want to give up the challenge, remain silent. It's up to you,' said Rao.

'A c . . . c . . . curse on anyone who remainsh sh . . . shilent,' said Khan Sahib after losing his train of thought. But by now he was finding it difficult to stand up. He was no longer in his senses. He began to sing loudly in a strange, coarse, frightening voice:

It'sh an infidel who proshtratesh himshelf, thinking it'sh a
    temple;
I've put my head down thinking it'sh the home of my
    beloved,
Thinking that'sh the home of my beloved, yesh, the home of
    my beloved . . .

And howling thus, he fell to the floor with a loud thump. People guffawed heartily, but Khan Sahib continued to raise the refrain of '*An infidel, yesh, an infidel . . .*' while prostrate.

Meanwhile, someone turned on the gramophone. Laughter, screams, loud chatter, dancing, cigarette smoke; a couple of men sitting quietly in the corner

watching the spectacle. A girl's dishevelled hair, her
desolate eyes; the adulation in that man's voice, the
sternness of his words; the group's initial delight
dissipated; it was now very late and it seemed as
though everyone was trying to be happy.

Naimuddin, who had returned by now, turned off
the gramophone. Then he announced, 'My landlady
says that there shouldn't be noise, or I'll have to
vacate the place.'

'That means we should now start heading home,'
said Rao.

'You live near my place, don't you? Come, we'll
walk together', 'May I drop you home in my car?'
and 'Certainly, thank you!'—such was the drift of the
conversations now.

Naim came up to Sheila, who was putting on her
coat as well.

'Are you going too?' he asked.

Sheila turned to look at Naim but did not answer.

'Do stay for a little while longer,' continued Naim.

'Very well,' she replied, walked towards the window,
and stood there.

Naim got busy seeing off his guests.

(II)

Arif and the girl with whom he had danced left
together. The fog had cleared; the electric lights were
gleaming fiercely in the cold winter wind. The trees
on the corner of the road stood silently, their branches
bare.

Arif felt cold. He was afraid he would catch a chill. It was not advisable to leave a closed, warm room and suddenly come out into the open like this. He was reminded of the Indian who caught pneumonia within a few days of arrival. If he came down with some illness of that sort, his entire career would be ruined.

'Mr Arif, where are we going?' asked the plump, beautiful girl.

This was all it took to convince Arif that the girl liked him. Glancing at her, he smiled triumphantly and responded, 'Why not walk someplace, have a cup of coffee and talk about it?'

'It's very late,' the girl replied in a tone which seemed to carry a hint of approval.

'We can walk to Lyon's Corner House; we'll get there in about ten to fifteen minutes. Since we've already spent so much time together, we might as well spend some more. Do come along,' said Arif.

They headed towards the Corner House.

Arif now began to plan all sorts of things in his mind. After coffee, he would take the girl to his room. But how? How would he begin a discussion on the subject with her? This was precisely the biggest obstacle in such matters. If only one could get a start, the entire business is easy. A start, a start—that's the most important thing!

'We've been together for an hour, but you still haven't told me what you do,' observed Arif.

'Who? Me? What do I do?' The girl laughed heartily.

'I often starve, although no one would ever presume that just by looking at me.'

What could this mean? Her clothes are so classy and she's so exquisitely dressed—looking at her, it seems she's in good circumstances. And she says she starves!

Arif tried to sympathize with her. 'I'm very sorry to hear this. But why don't you get a job?'

'I can't find one,' the girl replied, chuckling. 'I want to become an actress—a movie actress. I've been at it for three to four years, but I work only four or five times a month, and even then in very small, ordinary parts. How can I show my real talent in those? In my opinion, of all the jobs in the world, film acting is the most difficult. But, oh well, I don't care. In spite of these hurdles, I've made my life quite interesting. And then I say, what's to be gained by worrying? I have many friends, people like me— contented, unemployed. When we run out of our last shilling, we spend the entire night dancing in our room. I take a great interest in dancing, and I really like to do the rumba. I think I dance the rumba quite well. Do you enjoy dancing?' she suddenly asked Arif.

'Oh, yes. I take great interest in it, but have little time to pursue it,' he replied. What she said made him uncomfortable. He could not make out what sort of girl she was and did not know what to talk to her about. She was poor but happy nonetheless. What could that mean? She would dance when hungry— what's that?

'You seem to be one of those people who always read and write! Don't you ever feel restless? How do you spend your holidays? What do you do in your spare time, after all?' asked the girl, her face a picture of amazement. It appeared she had never met a young person of Arif's kind before.

'I'm preparing for a very difficult exam—the ICS exam. You've probably heard of it. It's the exam for the best jobs in India . . . but, oh well, I can certainly go dancing with you once a week,' he tried to sway the direction of the conversation to make the girl happy.

But she paid no attention to his efforts. She asked, 'ICS—what's that? Oh, now I understand. Civil service! Working in government offices. Back at home, when I was a child, I once knew an old man—a dry, withered character . . . and he always complained of indigestion! Why do you want to go into the civil service? I'm sure its a very boring, unremarkable sort of thing.'

Arif tried to explain. He maintained that the civil service was a completely different ball game in India. But it made no sense to the small-time actress. She said 'yes' and 'uh-huh' in a way that suggested she was losing interest in Arif. Arif's condition was peculiar. It was late and he was tired and growing increasingly irritated with the discussion. He felt angry—at the girl's stupidity, at his own lack of success. But the close proximity to that gorgeous woman fuelled his passions. The light scent of perfume;

the prominent bosom inside the tight coat; her lips, which were slightly plump but still lovely, like voluptuous grapes; and her large dark eyes, which appeared even darker in the night—Arif's senses were primed up only for these. The discussion, the road— in short, everything apart from this girl's youthful body—appeared immaterial.

They reached the rear of the British Museum. On one side, the University of London's new buildings were going up. Half-built walls, stairs, scaffolds, and stone-lifting cranes could be seen protruding from within a wooden enclosure; on the other side of the wide street, the museum's pillars stood tall, and at the centre of the platform below, two stone lions sat facing each other. At this time of night, there was complete solitude here. Arif reckoned that they would reach the Corner House in a few minutes. And then what kind of solitude would they find there? He mustered up some courage and placed his hand in the girl's. Then he squeezed it lightly. The girl responded by doing the same. Arif was elated. If the girl did not like him, why would she let him take her hand? Not only that, she had squeezed his hand as well. Arif could smell success.

But then he worried that she could be doing all this for money. It was apparent that she was not terribly impressed with Arif. Why this squeezing of his hand, then? Arif felt somewhat saddened by her poverty. What's the loss, he said to himself, if she gets some financial help as well? Money is spent on women in any case—be it one's wife or a prostitute, or some girl of this sort. Arif mustered up his courage. He glanced at the girl and exclaimed, 'How beautiful you are!'

'Really?' she said laughingly, as though the flattery did not have the slightest effect on her. And before Arif could say anything, she signalled towards the museum's lions and said, 'Do look at these! Have you ever noticed how old these lions seem? It's as though they don't even have teeth in their jaws. And they've only been here for eight or ten years. I have a friend—you really must meet him. He says that these lions are the image of British imperialism's decay, its impotence. They no longer have the pride of lions on their faces. It has been replaced by the venomousness of snakes. In my opinion, he's right. I, too, hate these lions. What do you think?'

'I've never observed them up close,' replied Arif worriedly. He was beginning to feel uneasy with the discussion. Politics, politics—wherever you go, the damned subject always comes up. Her friend must be some kind of communist; he must have filled this girl's head with these irrelevant thoughts. Otherwise, what does *she* have to do with British imperialism? He felt a strong resentment towards such people. Such individuals create trouble and mayhem everywhere. There's that Ahsan Sahib, who does not let any Indian student sit in peace in London. They think anyone who even contemplates getting a government job is a traitor. They consider Gandhi a slave of the capitalists. They believe even Jawaharlal to be weak because he follows Gandhi on sensitive issues. And here, in Europe, they do not consider anyone to be good. Baldwin, Lloyd George, MacDonald—they are all slaves of capitalists. And they are so arrogant that they begin to fancy themselves wiser than everyone else after reading the *Communist Manifesto*. A reproach for everything, criticizing everyone, finding faults in everything— that's all they are up to. What, after all, is wrong with these lions? But Arif did not have the courage to express his thoughts openly. He did not wish to say anything that would come across as unpleasant to the girl.

'Hooh!' said the girl softly, bringing Arif's chain of thought to a halt. Arif was now desperate to find a way to make the girl happy. The 'hooh' was uttered in a tone that suggested an uneasiness with his company.

'How nice your hair is,' Arif remarked with a smile.

'Really?' asked the girl in a dry tone. After this, silence. Arif felt ill at ease again; he wanted to embrace the girl, kiss her lips right there. How nice her lips seemed, and wasn't her body made to be held? It was quite possible that the girl herself wanted the same and was feeling bored with the conversation. Arif decided to ask her to come to his place when they sat down to have coffee. He was beginning to feel certain that she would agree. She's an actress, after all—she must live that kind of life.

In the meantime, they had reached Tottenham

Court Road. Even though it was late at night, this
stretch was full of bustle and activity. The cinema's
big shops and shining lights, policemen with long
black coats, a dance hall, some staggering drunks,
some people waiting at the bus stop. There were a
couple of newspaper sellers standing on one corner;
people moved about briskly. It was very cold.

The girl and Arif were just about to enter the
Corner House when she caught sight of a newspaper
seller standing on the other side of the street.

'I want to buy a *Daily Worker* for my friend; please
excuse me.' Saying this, she quickly crossed the street.

Arif remained standing where he was. Now he was
absolutely certain that it was the company of
communists that had ruined the girl; the newspaper
she went to buy was their newspaper. Its
advertisement was plastered on the wall nearby. A
GLORIOUS PROCESSION OF HUNGRY WORKERS. And on it
was the symbol of a red hammer and sickle.

Arif was displeased with the girl's sudden departure.
But she returned after a couple of minutes. She
understood that Arif was somewhat cross with her.

'Please forgive me, but I have a very close friend
who holds this newspaper in greater esteem than his
own life. I personally don't have much interest in
politics.'

'That's all right,' said Arif. He decided in his heart
that no matter what, he would rescue the girl from
the company of such undesirable elements. He had
begun to think of her as his property.

A bus stopped in front of them. Seeing it, the girl leaped up. 'Oh, this is my bus; it'll take me straight to my place; you wouldn't mind if I left right now, would you? There won't be another bus after this one; you'd have to take me home in a taxi; you'll save money,' she said in a single breath, and before Arif could respond, she boarded the vehicle. 'Goodbye,' she cheerfully called out to Arif from the footboard of the bus.

'Goodbye!' replied Arif softly. The bus departed; he remained standing where he was. Regret, helplessness and anger writ large on his countenance. He felt the sorrowful recognition of his solitude. The girl's laughing figure swirled in front of his eyes. Now, he could not think of other women, but as far as the girl was concerned, he had no hope of meeting her ever again. He did not even know her address, and now it was abundantly clear that she was not in the least interested in him. He remained standing there for some time, and then, hailing a taxi, headed home.

(III)

'I don't understand you at all,' said Rao to Ahsan. 'On the one hand, you criticize the Indian students here so much that you make them seem like the world's most contemptible creatures; on the other, you also expect them to become your comrades, and that, with no thought of personal gain, they should understand the problems of their country and the world and take part in big movements. In my opinion, this is stupidity. We're completely useless. Our minds are incapable of anything new or innovative. There is nothing but intellectual and spiritual death. These people have neither the ability to come up with a fresh thought, nor the strength to stand by the truth.'

Rao and Ahsan were walking home from Naimuddin's place. They lived in the same flat.

'Your logic always takes you to the sort of sheltered space where sitting idle appears to be the best thing to do,' replied Ahsan. 'The Indian students here are specimens of India's wealthy class and, according to the majority of people, this class is certainly the sort which has no good left in it. Take the big rajas, nawabs and noblemen. Does their ilk benefit anybody? These parasites don't even know how to spend their own wealth on themselves properly. They are absurd even in their extravagance; their heads are full of crap. There is only one thing they know how to do well: selling off the nation. And for this blessed work, they can make big sacrifices.

'What's left are middle-class people. There are many among them who're alive because of the good graces of such noblemen. For instance, lawyers, barristers, government servants, or tycoons, moneylenders, capitalists. They are certainly sensible people, but their only aim is to amass wealth. Just as a prostitute sells her body for money, these people sell their mental abilities; still, it cannot be denied that these people have great qualities. In my opinion, their special attribute is their spinelessness. Just as ancient man, in his ignorance, fancied demons behind every tree and rock, these people are undone by an all-encompassing fear—hemmed in as they are by enemies on all sides. Fear of the government, fear of rajas and maharajas, fear of religion, fear of mullahs, fear of Brahmins.

'If one is a government servant, he sits ever so meekly in front of his officer, like a dog with its tail between its legs. But when the tables are turned and he is the one in control, his treatment of those below him is beyond inhumane: threats, rebukes—he won't talk but intimidate and browbeat. Whether it's a lawyer, a moneylender, a merchant or a capitalist, they all keep hoping that their colleagues will fail, be ruined, and that all their rivals' wealth will be transferred to them.

'Even so, all these people continue to fear those from a class lower than their own. Fear that the labourer will stop working for them, that the farmer will begin to say that the land belongs to the one who cultivates it, that the order of things will be reversed! Over and over, these people find solace in the fact that India isn't Russia, but the rising power of communism will no longer let them sit in peace. They see the demon of communism in every progressive movement. It's the sons of these very people who come to Europe for an education. What, then, can we expect of them?'

'I think the same thing! So why are you getting angry with me?' asked Rao.

'Because just *saying* this isn't enough,' replied Ahsan quickly. 'Don't we see with our own eyes every day that individuals of this very class, after relinquishing the benefits of their caste and exclusive group, not only back India's oppressed, but wholeheartedly become one with them? And by leaving the cowardliness of their class altogether, they become immersed in the sort of revolutionary mentality which gives them an iron will and the strength of steel? The reason for this is that these few individuals understand very well that, from a historical perspective, the class to which they were born has now run its course. It has received its death warrant because its existence is an obstacle on the path of the human race. But this change, this understanding, doesn't come about suddenly; it's the result of years of mental and physical toil. It's easy for the worker to understand that the fruit of his labour should go to him. But it's very difficult for the wealthy man to understand this—not because it is a complicated idea, but because it will harm him.

'For the most part, it's from among these students that one or two people will be prepared to act on these revolutionary principles on behalf of workers and labourers. Wouldn't it be a big mistake if we don't even try to help such students along that path—students who show the capacity to accept our new ideas, whose hearts haven't died, whose minds

haven't decayed, and whose bodies don't shy away
from work? We ought to lead them along the path
where the lights of life are found, where there are
afflictions, and problems, and difficulties, no doubt,
but not the pitch-black darkness of death. Where the
name of every absurd, senseless thing isn't happiness,
but where there's a new sense of joy—the joy of
overpowering the blind powers of nature; the joy of
taking people out of the barbarity of ignorance, chaos
and selfishness, and creating a stable, civilized and
enlightened world; the joy of work; the joy of labour
and toil.'

Ahsan fell quiet. Rao too did not respond. They
continued walking in silence for some time. Then Rao
said softly, 'You're right. But what can be done?
These people can't even bear *listening* to your words.
How will you change their thinking? These students
are occupied only with getting a job and making a
livelihood. And the few who do listen to you are like
me: they listen, understand, and forget. Or if they're
very interested, they wear a red tie and attend some
socialist meeting, and read a couple of books on the
subject—that's all. But there's absolutely no change
in their lifestyle. Why is this? Sometimes I ask myself:
Why is it, though I do sympathize with your thoughts,
that I don't ever join you in doing some real work?
There's a strange sort of mental apathy that envelops
us, just as a light fire burning over a feverish body
eventually reduces it to ashes. I feel that the soul,
too, has a similar sickness which first slowly disengages
our spirit, then kills it off.'

'Oh well, it's good enough that you perceive that such a sickness exists. Those who don't have a perception of this are the truly despicable ones.'

'If such people had that perception in them, we wouldn't call them corpses now, would we?'

(IV)

Reaching his room, Azam turned on the gas heater. He removed his hat, threw it on the bed and, without taking off his overcoat, sat on the chair near the fireplace. Nothing could be seen too well—it was dark. On one side was a small bookshelf on the wall; beneath it a table. There were a couple of chairs, a bed in the corner. The room was very small, and the table and chair appeared to be piled high with an assortment of things.

In this darkness, Azam thought of the alleys of India's cities—Delhi, Lucknow, Benares—where there is complete darkness at night, or very little light. Once, late in the night, he was going to the market with his friend. It was pitch dark. A stench arose from the gutters. As they walked, they spotted a light peeping out of the door of an apartment. Looking more closely, they saw two old men facing each other on a bed; their bodies were adorned with nothing except flimsy loincloths and their white beards; they were bent low over a chess mat laid out in front of them. It seemed as if only these two old men were awake in the big city, and that all the lights in the

city had been extinguished, save for their lantern.
Azam and his friend remained standing for some
time, but the old men did not even lift their heads to
look in their direction. Thinking about them right
now made Azam somewhat happy. Why was it so? he
wondered. Why had this old memory, laden with
layers of the dust of time, sprung to his mind now?
Then he thought of the friend who had been with
him. He had not received news of him for three years.
After passing his BA, the friend had tried to find a
job, but had been unsuccessful. His name was
Bishamber. At the time, he had been married. He
would now have kids as well. Perhaps he lived in
some village now. He did not have the money to
study for an LLB. Bishamber's wife and children
must be in difficulty. Unemployment was on the rise.
How would things turn out? How will things turn out
for me? Will I pass my exams? If I do, will I find a
job? And the people who died of bullets; what will
become of their wives and children?

Azam thought of his little sister, who was around
twelve years old. This week he had received a letter
from her in which she wrote: *We're all waiting anxiously
for your return. Come soon. Mother prays for your
success all the time and says that she's picked out a very
nice bride for you.* But he had absolutely no desire to
go back. He certainly did want to be reunited with
his elderly parents and young siblings, but his initial
desire to return home quickly after passing his exams
was no longer there. Mother has picked out a nice

bride for me. He began to laugh at the very thought. Why not? After all, this has been going on not only in India but throughout the world for hundreds of years. Everything here is for the market. Why shouldn't I do what others do? But love? Passion? Is there room for these in our culture? His thoughts went over the evening's events again, and then he remembered the beginning of his love.

Is *this* 'love'? The first time he met Jean, they ate together at a party. There were fifteen or twenty other people—both men and women—present as well, but his eyes were fixed on this one girl. Many days later, she came here for the first time. It was this same room. She was sitting on this chair. Then I sat her on my lap and kissed her. After this, he began to recall other days, other nights. He tried to think of something else. Remembering past joys can be very painful.

He suddenly stood up and switched on the lights. His glance fell on the lifesize mirror on the closet door. He caught a glimpse of himself. His stubble had grown a bit, and there were dark bags under his eyes. He turned away from the mirror and began to undress.

How nice it would be if Jean had come with me today. No, no—even as I try not to, I can't get her out of my thoughts. How nice she looked today. But what's it to me? What's it to me? Oh, how hard life is! If only I could think of something else. Paris. People say that one can get rid of all sorrows in Paris. Not true. A mistake, a coincidence. A mistake *and* a coincidence—the perfect recipe for misfortune and distress. But where do I wish to go?

He put on his nightclothes. He was feeling tired. He stretched his limbs, switched the light off, and jumped into bed. His blanket felt ice-cold. He began to shiver. But the bed warmed up soon, and he spread his feet, then changed his position.

I had to put up with such cold this evening at the Russell Square station . . . it was so insulting too. Good thing it was Rao I met. Jean. Of course, I did dance with her tonight, but I didn't feel the same happiness I felt when I first met her. Happiness? The real paradise is the one we've lost. Whose words are these? A French novelist. Desire, attempt, striving— these are all merely words, ones which relate to the future, and that's why they're useless. But memories don't provide any joy either. What are memories? They are so different from reality, which offers an opportunity for happiness and which, after a few days, lingers on like a fragrance or memory. Both are completely different things, yet still one. Being alone in this world is so terrible as well.

If only Jean were here with me right now. Why did she leave after all? Paris . . . how great it would be if I were there right now. Those same women that I saw then would be there. What an idiot I was back then. I spent a hundred francs on absolutely nothing. Completely naked women. One of them held my hand and placed it on her chest. I ran from there. It was a dark alley, and there was a red lamp on the door. Rao says that France is notorious for no reason. Which place has no defects? There is, yes, less hypocrisy among the French than others. I don't know ...

Jean, how did you get here? You and Paris? How did you manage to find time to come and see me today? Is it because you're afraid of my dear mother that you don't come to see me? Silly girl! I have a lot of money. I'm not dependant on my parents. Why have you taken off your clothes? Don't you feel cold? Come, will you play chess with me? This music's playing so loudly. I don't like it. You won't go back now, will you ... stay here. Now don't ever go away from me ... this is my little sister. Do come and meet her ...

7

Sheila and Naim were left alone in the room. Dirty glasses, empty bottles, bits of smoked cigarettes, and full ashtrays; plates—some empty, some with crumbs of bread and biscuits—were scattered here and there. The gramophone had stopped playing, but it, too, was left open on a table. Records were scattered all around it, on the table and chair. The flame in the fireplace was close to burning out. The room was filled with cigarette smoke, and the air felt heavy.

Naim said to Sheila, 'Please make yourself comfortable.' Sheila was near the window. Naim went and stood near her.

'I can't breathe here. If you don't mind, please open these curtains and the windows. This room needs fresh air.'

Naim opened the windows and glanced at the street below. Complete silence. He remained standing there, his head out of the window, for some time. Sheila came up to him and began looking outside as well. The sky had cleared, and from behind the roofs of the houses, a half-moon, a yellowish moon whose

light disappeared as it reached the ground, could be
seen.

'The moon seems so vast in London. It can be seen
here, but there's no moonlight.'

Naim did not reply. A taxi pulled up on the street
below and, reaching the front of the next house,
stopped. A woman and a man got out. After hugging
each other, they kissed. Then the woman ran into the
house, and the man got into the taxi and left. Silence
descended on the street again. Sheila and Naim left
the window and went near the fireplace. Naim sat on
a chair. Sheila remained standing near the fire.

'I should go home now.'

'Sit, sit for a little while,' said Naim in a voice at
once harsh and pleading.

Sheila said nothing; she looked tired. She sat down.
After some time, she remarked, 'That was some party!'

'I hope you didn't feel uncomfortable. Strange types
of men showed up.'

'No, not at all. In fact, I was very happy to meet
you. But now I'm rather tired. It's very late.'

'You must be wondering why I was so insistent on
your staying behind. Everyone's left and you must be
sleepy as well. But I don't know why I can't sleep;
and not only that, I feel a storm has erupted in my
heart and mind—the way a storm accompanies the
rains in India; when dark clouds gather and make the
night even darker, and when lightning flashes over
and over again in this darkness, and the sky trembles
with fear from one end to the other.' Naim fell silent
and looked towards Sheila.

'Please do me a favour and don't talk about such things, Naim.' Sheila's face was a picture of sorrow.

'Why not?'

'Because I like you a lot. But I love someone else.' She continued to speak in a very faint voice. 'He, too, was an Indian student, and we were in love with each other.'

A strange commotion broke out in Naim's heart. Emotions of love, sympathy and envy tormented and confounded him. He wanted to forget himself somehow—to save himself from the storm of his desires, miseries and sorrows in some way.

'Who was he? When did you meet him? And where is he now?' Naim asked spontaneously.

Sheila looked at him. Then she lay down on the chair. 'Oh god, I won't go crazy, will I? It's been a year and a half! Letters used to come at first; now they don't. Now there's no one in the world I can talk to about him ... You ask who he was. Listen. This is what happened some years ago ...

'There's a small village on the edge of a blue lake in the Swiss mountains; there were altogether maybe twenty-five or thirty houses when I visited the place. How can I forget it? It was summer. The month of July, and how pleasant the season was! The sunshine was like moonlight; the sky a deep blue. Small white patches of clouds drifted slowly like puffs of cotton. The snow on the peaks of distant mountains would shine like milk. In some places, patches of clouds—stuck to the foot of the mountains like a herd of white

sheep—would hide the snow. Beneath the high peaks
you could see deep valleys, on which descended a
shade . . .

'I was sitting alone under the sunshade of a café,
drinking tea. A young Indian man was sitting nearby.
I glanced in his direction; then I began looking at the
lovely mountains and the spectacle of sunshine and
shade on them. A couple of minutes later, he got up
and left. On his way out he glanced at me as well. I
turned my face away. Our first meeting! How do such
coincidences take place in our lives? And then why do
the pace and direction of our lives change because of
them? There was no trace of him for the next two
days. Only his thick black hair, large eyes, slender
lips, and smallish nose; and that colour of his face,
sunburnt, like copper: these would spin around in my
head from time to time. A vague memory that would
occasionally flash before me, and nothing more. On
the third day, I was roaming around the edge of the
lake. Suddenly I saw him approaching. Seeing me, a
light smile lit up his face and he nodded. Had he
greeted me? I didn't reply. He quickly moved away
from where I was. I felt that I'd been extremely rude.
This is why Indians hate us. He had greeted me and
instead of acknowledging it, I had turned my face
away. I began to think: What should I do to put
things right? It's such a small thing; it'll seem strange
even if I meet him and apologize. The sorts of follies
one commits when nervous! And now he'll begin to
hate me!

'That same day, I saw him again in the evening.
After dinner, I left my tiny hotel and stood alone,
looking in the direction of the snowy mountains. The
sun had gone down, and the sky was awash with the
many shades of light. A cast of red lay on the snow.
I sensed that someone had come and stood near me.
I turned to look. The same young man! He wasn't
still angry with me, was he? After some time I said,
"What a nice sight."

'"Yes, what a nice sight."

'I didn't know what to make of this reply. He
wasn't making fun of me, was he? Was he being
sarcastic? Or perhaps he had conveyed his actual
opinion. Maybe he wasn't cross with me and had
forgotten about the incident that happened earlier
during the day.

'"You're staying at this hotel, right? I've been
seeing you for a number of days," he said a little
later.

'I was elated. I laughed a little at the way he spoke
English.

'"Yes! I've been staying here for three days. I've
seen you a number of times here and there, too," I
replied.

'After this, a series of exchanges began. We would
talk as though we had known each other for ages. He
told me that he was studying medicine in London,
and that it was his final year. He would be going
back home the next year. He had come to the small
Swiss village for a month. He was from Bengal and

his name was Pal, Hiren Pal. I told him my name as well, and said that I, too, had come to Switzerland for my holidays.

'That night, I went to a coffee house. The village's coffee house, restaurant, dance hall—it was all of these. A long room with a low ceiling, its wooden roof and floor gave off a pleasant aroma. Tables were spread all about. Around each of these tables were three or four chairs. On one side, on a dais, a pianist, a drummer and a violinist were playing. People were sitting here and there, speaking all of Europe's languages. It was a large crowd. Nearly all the tables were occupied and crammed close to each other. There was one empty table in a corner, though. I sat down to have my coffee there.

'After a short while, I saw Hiren come in. He looked around to find a place. Then his glance fell upon me; I, too, was looking in his direction. Our eyes met, and he immediately came near my table and, without asking for permission, pulled out a chair and sat next to me.

'Whether or not this displeased me, I don't know to this day. But when I looked towards him and found him so close, I forgot these minor points of etiquette. We sat talking for hours. Time passed quickly—very quickly. An Englishman was sitting near our table— red face, small, thin moustache. I could see that he felt an uncontrollable rage at seeing me sitting with a young Indian man. But I didn't care at all. Hiren, too, paid no attention to him.

'I don't remember very well the things I spoke to Hiren about that night. Perhaps there was no subject in the world that we didn't discuss. The only thing I remember very well is that I said a couple of things which I felt embarrassed about no sooner than I had uttered them. But I kept talking, without thinking or understanding. Hiren kept asking me questions. He would respond to my answers; sometimes he'd laugh at me; sometimes correct my mistakes; on occasion, even if I was in agreement with him, I'd interrupt him in the middle of a sentence, just to listen to his answer or to try and prove him wrong. He would raise his eyebrows immediately; a flash of lightning would brighten his eyes; a sharpness, warmth and zeal would materialize in his voice. When he spoke like this, it would be difficult for me to listen. I'd remain gazing steadfastly at him! Seeing my reaction, he, too, would stop talking in mid-sentence and begin smiling.

'That night, I lay awake for a long time, relishing the discussion. Hiren's voice rang in my ears, and his laughter, the flash in his dark eyes, his smile circled in front of my eyes. My heart was filled with a strange joy.

'We would go on walks, play tennis, swim in the lake, and have our meals together. We didn't know anyone in the village. Staying together like this all the time, we got to know each other in a way that normally takes people months.

'I began to like everything about him, and felt that

I hadn't ever met a nicer man. To me, he was the most interesting, attractive and likeable person I had ever known. I recall that I had expressed these very thoughts in a letter I had written at the time to my friend Doris. And she wrote back: *Sheila! You've fallen in love, be careful! It's summer, the time when the blood of youth sometimes rushes to the head and makes us crazy. I'm not stopping you from going crazy—that's your right. But don't forget that your "obsession" could be a lasting one. He could make your life or ruin it . . .*

'After receiving Doris's letter, I kept asking myself: Is it true that my heart has set itself on this young man? I like him; I want to talk to him; I want to be close to him—but love, passion? Is this what they call love? Is this passion? Some days those were—I didn't worry about a thing. My world was separate from everyone else's, and even the thought of escaping its magic circle would not cross my mind.

'Then one night I was sitting in his room, talking to him. It was rather warm. He opened the window. It was completely silent outside. Stray rays of light filtered through the leaves of the trees from the street below. Still, dim outlines of trees adorned the mountaintops, and the mountains themselves appeared like lumps of darkness. But the sky was completely clear, and in it gleamed hundreds of thousands of shining stars.'

Sheila stopped.

Naim did not say anything either. He was thinking: What should I say? Why, after all, is this wounding of the heart, this anguish, written in man's destiny? What can I do? How helpless we are. The most painful spiritual predicament is one that disarms us, closes its doors to all our efforts and exertions and entangles our emotions . . .

Sheila lay back on her chair as though she had fallen asleep. Naim rose suddenly and came near her chair. He kept looking at her. Sheila remained lying there. Naim hurriedly turned his face away and stood near the fireplace.

Sheila said, 'No, Naim. No. You and I can't untie this knot. I believe there are degrees of joy as well. When we end up losing all possibilities of our personal, limited happiness, and our hearts become so desolate that nothing remains in them besides the ghosts of memories, we have to leave these ruins behind. Life is ever-flowing; it always appears before us in new manifestations, and now it requires us to go to a higher plane, and, from there, search for more happiness, more extensive joys, which are not limited only to our person, but which all of humanity can partake of . . .'

But for Sheila, those ruins were not desolate. She knew that this was a story that would come to an end. She used to think that the world of reality was separate from this story, but at this moment, Naim, this room, her present life, appeared artificial and fake. Only that night was real.

'We went near the window and stood there. Hiren and I. He turned off the light. The scenery outside,

the room's darkness, and Hiren's proximity to me—
I felt intoxicated. Hiren slowly placed his hand on
my back and embraced me. I was scared and unable
to utter a single word. Hiren, too, remained completely
silent. I kept struggling with him, but he kept kissing
me with a brutish ecstasy. The only thing he would
say from time to time would be "My beauty, my
love". How meaningful those words were at the time.
Eventually, I broke free. He reached for me but I
opened the door, ran straight for my room, took a
deep breath and, reaching there, began to sob. My
tears continued to flow despite my efforts. My heart,
mind, body—every part of my being experienced a
strange, tingling sensation. I fell asleep. I had probably
never slept so soundly before.

'After this, we became like one soul in two bodies.
It was either because of the beauty of the place with
its magnificent mountains, or the season playing its
tricks, or, perhaps, the springs of hidden, eternal joy
within both of us that had come to a boil. I felt as if
I was in the midst of a strange magical atmosphere.'

Sheila continued, 'Have you ever gone on a hike
into the mountains? On foot? Walking uphill for
miles among pine trees, waterfalls, and deep valleys?'
She stopped for a moment. Naim turned and gazed at
her, but said nothing. It was as if Sheila was talking
to herself. 'Near the lake was a narrow road—some
two yards wide or even less—which led up to the top
of the mountains. Large pine trees shaded all about.
Sunlight through the leaves fell on the road and on

the mountains. This road would gradually become steeper and steeper so that after a half hour of walking, one would be drenched in sweat. But one would reach such a great height that, from there, people strolling at the side of the lake would appear absolutely tiny and the houses would look like playhouses. A light wind was blowing, and from the delicate, pointy needles of the pine trees, a soft and deep rustling could be heard—the kind of noise that increases the sense of disparity between the magnificence of mountains, their solitude, and the struggles and conflicts of the world.

'This road looped around the foot of the mountain like a fine thread. On one side a deep ravine, on the other, a mountain, like a magnificent wall of stone which giants must have begun building to reach the sky. But there were fissures, crevices and caves in several places. Boulders sat upon those fissures and on levelled surfaces. These boulders would have a reddish moss on top, or would be completely smooth, like a man's shining bald head. All around and beneath them, near the roots of large trees, small flowers—blue, white, pink—had sprung up, resembling a group of children who had strayed into a gathering of old men, their cheeks red from embarrassment and their eyes bent to the ground.

'I remember quite well that it must have been approaching three o'clock. I was going up this road with Hiren. Both of us huffed and puffed as we sluggishly took huge steps and made our way forward.

With every step, we took a deep breath, which made
it seem as if we'd been walking for a long time. We
were carrying sticks in our hands, and wearing big
boots; we were walking in complete silence. After a
few minutes, we came upon an opening along the
road where there were no big trees near the chasm
and you could see the entire valley below. The sunlight
here was intense. Both of us stopped and, turning
towards the opening, stood there. Before our eyes was
a strange sight.

'Enclosed by the mountains, we beheld a valley
hundreds of yards below, and between it the same
lake from which we had come walking. The sun's rays
were shining only on one part of the lake, which was
gleaming like mercury; the shaded portion was a
deep, darkish-blue. In one corner of the lake, where
there was sunshine, we saw a crowd of people bathing;
from the distance, they appeared to be crawling like
ants. Large, multicoloured umbrellas had been driven
into the ground. People lay under them, enjoying the
shade. We could see a few hotels from there; their
rooms appeared exactly like dovecotes. One mountain
on the other side of the valley was peculiar: half its
bottom was filled with trees, but these decreased
higher up, towards the top. In their place were small
shrubs, scattered about. And very near the summit
lay brown rocks, a line of projecting peaks, like the
sharp teeth of a comb. Behind this mountain, as far
as the eye could see, there were more mountains—
row upon row of peaks touching the sky. In the far

horizon, hidden in a light-blue cloud of dust, you could see a series of snow-capped peaks where the gleam of the sun and the shade blended the white of the snow and the blue of the sky to create before one's eyes such a complete picture of colour, light, darkness, magnificence and loftiness that it's impossible to convey its beauty.

'A strange silence cast itself over us! Without uttering a word, both of us kept looking at this sight for a minute or two. In the midst of these trees, rocks, mountains, and beneath this sky and clouds, we had become totally absorbed in the deep solitude.

'"We should hurry," urged Hiren, turning towards me, "or it will be late." And saying this, he moved forward.

'I turned as well. "Yes, we should hurry," I repeated slowly and moved forward.

'His eyes, those Indian eyes—I liked those above all else. Their shining darkness and with it their softness . . . I thought to myself: This isn't a weakness, is it? But when he spoke to me about India and the work that he would do there, the softness of these eyes would disappear. Grief would flash in them sometimes and at times they would breathe fire.

'We continued climbing up the mountain with long strides. The sound of our boots could be heard on the stony road. Suddenly, my heart began to sink. How would this love of ours turn out? This question began to plague my mind. Just as children are afraid of ghosts in the dark, I began to feel afraid. It sometimes

happens, doesn't it, that the lamp of happiness goes
out all at once?

'"Hiren, do you really love me?"

'Hiren stopped suddenly, began laughing and,
without answering the question, grabbed my hand,
pulled me towards him, and embraced me. "Of course
not! How *can* I love you? What do we have in
common? I'm black; you're white. I'm Indian; you're
English. I'm an idol worshipper; you're a Christian.
And on top of all of that, my heart is filled with
hatred, not only for you, but for the entire English
nation. Hatred—warm, boiling hatred! So, my dear,
you judge for yourself. How can I love you?"

'Both of us began laughing, and the matter was put
to rest. We continued walking.

'After a short while, Hiren said, "But to tell you
the truth, I never imagined that I'd get stuck this
badly in the web of love in Europe. And now I see
only you all about me."

'I felt a limitless happiness, but said, "No, this isn't
right. I don't believe what you say. You've already
chosen the purpose of your life and it is dearer to you
than I am."

'"Will we never have the same opinion on this
matter?" asked Hiren in a sorrowful tone. "Why do
you repeatedly try to get me to say that the circle of
life isn't limited to love and passion? Aren't there
many other problems, interesting and uninteresting
things, to which we are bound? We can't leave these
things and love each other in a vacuum. Just as air

is necessary for life, the love we share depends—at least to my thinking—upon striving to obtain those purposes, which you say I hold dearer than I do you. My dear! There's no contradiction, no quarrel between you and these objectives. Your love makes me more courageous. Life still appears difficult to me, but with you by my side, I will easily walk this arduous path. I can only promise you one thing, and it is this: As far as it lies in my power, I'll never leave your side on this path. But you, are you absolutely certain that you're prepared to walk with me?"

'I can't forget his words. His voice reverberates in my ears. I replied in ecstasy, "I'm prepared to go anywhere, in any direction with you—whatever path it might be, no matter the road. If you're with me, I'll keep moving forward fearlessly. Like right now!" But the joy of love in my heart seemed, for reasons which didn't make sense to me, clouded with an inexplicable grief.

'Silence cast itself upon us again. A piece of a cloud drifted in front of the sun, and the sunlight was blocked. All about, a thick forest of tall pine trees. All around the road, piled on top of each other, lay brown, pointed, dry pine needles; walking on them made one's foot slip. They were giving off a scent. With the clouds gathering, it became dark there as well.

'We had just arrived near a bend when we spotted an old Swiss guide approaching. He was wearing a small green hat. His face was the deep reddish colour characteristic of those who spend their lives outdoors, buffeted by the wind and the sun. On his cheeks and forehead were dark, black, pockmarks. But the old man appeared powerful. On his back was a climbing rope and a clock; in his hand was a stick, a little over a yard long, which had thick iron spikes on each end, straight at the bottom and bent on top. As he came near, he greeted us with a smile.

"'Gut' tag!" he said in a Swiss-German accent.

"'Good day!" we replied in unison.

'Then the man paused for a moment and asked, "Are you two going to Zeiler? Hurry or you'll get caught in the storm. The colour of the sky doesn't look good."

'We paused as well. Hiren asked the guide in his broken German, "How long will it take us to get to Zeiler from here?"

"'About two hours, if you walk quickly. There's no place to take refuge along the way. If it begins to rain, it won't be possible to escape getting drenched."

"'We'll try to walk faster. Thank you very, very much for warning us," I said.

'We said goodbye to the guide and began climbing the slope at a quicker pace.

"'If only I were a guide in Switzerland," said Hiren, taking a deep breath.

"'Why?" I asked immediately.

"'So I could be close to the blind forces of nature! Storms, rain, snow, speedy winds, cold—getting acquainted with all of these and struggling with them, overpowering them. What more could one wish for?"

'"But one needn't spend an entire lifetime in the mountains in order to bring these powers under one's control!"

'"Absolutely not. Scientists can work sitting cooped up in their laboratories, but my temperament isn't of that sort. I want to feel the gust of stormy gale and listen to the shriek of the winds coursing through the mountains. The way the tall trees sway back and forth as if drunk, the helpless rustle of leaves—I like all of this too . . . But you! I like you more than all of these!"

'I replied with a laugh, "Then why don't you become a guide? It isn't that difficult."

'"Perhaps because it *isn't* difficult! The time to become a guide hasn't come yet. Man is still prey to blind forces in his everyday business. Right now we need to fight a war against these human forces. Once that battle is won, we'll have complete leave to engage in combat with the forces of nature according to our individual capacities and liking."

'I continued to tease him. "You speak as if the burden of all of mankind's problems and afflictions is on your shoulders alone!"

'He quickly replied, "No. But the burden of some of these hardships is certainly on my shoulders. I only want to try and lessen it. If all of us understood this, more than half the battle would be won. But forget this for the moment. Right now I only want to think of you and you alone!"

'We continued talking in the same vein and climbing the mountain. The more we moved forward, the narrower the road became. There were places where only two people could pass, with difficulty. It was an arduous climb; stones were scattered about everywhere. In certain places, the rocky ground jutted out like half a roof. In spite of our efforts and because of the slope and the steepness, our feet moved slowly. And my heart was heavy with a weight that seemed to have been mixed in love, as clouds in wind. It was difficult to separate one from the other.

'How distant that day feels today! I had everything, but I kept feeling that I wasn't as happy as I used to be. The question would repeatedly come up in my heart: Are the cracks beginning to show? And I would answer myself: No. Absolutely not. Then what was it, after all?

'I would repeatedly think: What would the outcome of this limitless love be? Hiren wanted to take me to India with him. What if this wasn't possible for some reason?

'Hiren was poor; he'd need to earn money. Without it, how would we be able to live in India? And I'm poor as well. I'd say in my heart: If only I were rich! Then I'd think: I don't have confidence in my precious love; I don't have faith in Hiren. Oh god, I am so riddled with doubt!

'The man I was prepared to give my life and sacrifice everything for—how could I nurture doubt about him in my heart! I'm in love with this young

man. I'm deeply in love with him. I knew nothing
more than that. My mind refused to work at all at the
time. Have you ever perceived the magnificent silence
of the mountains, Naim? There's a strange, enticing
dread in it. How silent it was at that time, how still!
Only the sound of our walking, the clatter of leather
on stone roads. The air had thinned out as well, and
the clouds piled overhead . . .

'I looked at Hiren and said, "Hiren!"'

'"What is it, Sheila?"'

'"Talk to me. I want to hear your voice."'

'He glanced at me lovingly and, putting his hand in
mine, said, "I'll talk to you about whatever you order
me to speak about."'

'"Whatever you feel like. All right, then. India.
Speak of your country," I replied. Hiren had often
talked to me about India's social and political issues.

'He began: "What can I tell you about that country?
Where I come from, everything that is good and bad
in the world exists in the extreme. No, that's wrong.
What I *should* say is that everything that's good in
the world has the potential of finding its limit in
India but all that is bad has already found a haven.

'"You must have heard people say that 'spirituality'
has a great influence in India. That's a complete lie.
There can be two meanings of 'spirituality': one, the
opposition to 'materialism'—that is, not worrying
about material things, stressing religiosity, worship,
and preferring to talk about the afterlife rather than
worldly things."

'"And what's the other meaning of spirituality?" I asked.

'"The other could mean fighting—within this wordly life—greed, ambition, the use of force and oppression on others, ignorance, irrationality, dishonesty, and awakening the sleeping melodies of life which, in order to be heard, require from us a big heart, an open mind and a vigorous body. Both types of spirituality are totally lacking where I come from."

'I teased, "You used to be a pretty big materialist. What made you think of spirituality today?"

'"I *am* a materialist, but only so that I can help in the realization of man's mental and spiritual progress. Today, people who harp on spirituality don't even have a distant relationship with it. What *is* spirituality? The mind steeped in culture!" He continued, "You must have read in the newspapers about how, where I come from, Hindus and Muslims and Sikhs fight each other because of religion. But does this mean that they're filled with spirituality or religiosity? Absolutely not. In order to get government positions solely for their personal benefit, some religious leaders who have all but forgotten God make the naive and the poor fight each other in the name of religion. They have nothing to do with religion or spirituality.

'"What's left is the other type of spirituality. In a nation that's enslaved—in which eighty per cent of the population doesn't have enough food to eat; disease, plague, sickness are so rampant that it's difficult to see a healthy person in the entire country; where education is limited to a handful of people; where even children are like withered flowers; where hunger, starvation, poverty and affliction can be seen written on the faces of most people, and laziness, stupidity, ignorance and a loathsome kind of contentment on the rest—to search for the light of spirituality is entirely stupid."

"'You're exaggerating. There must certainly be people besides these who perceive such things and who are striving to bring about changes," I replied.

'Hiren laughed. He said, "Yes, this probably seems like an exaggeration to you because you can't place me in any of these categories. There's another, third type where I come from: those who pontificate. Such people are wise. There's not a problem in the world they can't get to the bottom of. They have the power of distinguishing between right and wrong. They understand the reality of all things, the reason behind everything. But that's it: after getting there, they're incapable of doing anything. They have the power to understand the world, but not the power to change it. They haven't joined the life-giving revolutionary struggle of millions of India's hardworking people. Their condition is the most lamentable. These victims of cowardliness, indolence, laziness and mental jadedness, they too can be counted in the company of lazy people and good-for-nothings in the end . . . "

"'It seems that hopelessness has overpowered you today; that's why you're talking like this," I noted.

'A little later we arrived at our destination, Zeiler. Here, on top of a lofty mountain, there was only one small hotel with six or seven rooms. There was a veranda, some eight to ten yards long and three or four yards wide, enclosed with glass on three sides.

'It was close to six o'clock. Black clouds were gathering, and it was getting darker. The location was so beautiful that one forgot the difficult climb of three and a quarter hours. A valley resembling a reservoir and, at its bottom, a green meadow. In the middle of it, a small, rapidly flowing river. The surrounding mountains didn't appear so high here. Snow rested on their peaks. Waterfalls careened from above with great force and noise, the sound reverberating all around the valley. The waterfall in the middle was the largest. It fell from an elevation of some thirty or forty yards, its water crashing down onto the rocks and becoming a tumultuous river; flowing from there, it disappeared into the valley.

'We were alone in the hotel at that time and sat at a table which had an excellent view.

'We were famished with all that walking. The waitress, a plump, young Swiss country girl, brought tea, bread, butter and jam, and we began eating and drinking.

'In the meantime, it had begun raining and darkness spread outside.

'"It would be better if we stayed here today," said Hiren. "It would be impossible to go back in the rain now." But why, after all, am I saying all these things

to you? What's happened to me? I can't seem to stop
blabbering. Give me a cigarette, Naim.'

Naim reached out and handed Sheila a cigarette,
and she began smoking. A blue veil cast itself around
her face. She became immersed in her thoughts.

Naim said, 'Sheila, is there a remedy for us? How
painfully ironic that both of us stand helpless in the
face of tumultuous waves in this stormy ocean of
emotions, like two boats without a sail, but cannot
help each other at all. Poor Sheila!'

But Sheila looked as if she had fallen asleep on her
chair. She was recalling that stormy night in Zeiler.
That night of love and sorrow, when her eyes opened
in the middle of sleep, and she had whispered in a
faint, weak voice, 'Hiren, my dear Hiren', waking
him up.

'Why, what's the matter?' he had asked with a
start.

'Hold me tight, close to you, I'm scared,' she had
answered.

Hiren had embraced her tightly and kissed her lips
and her eyes repeatedly.

'My love, my dearest Sheila!'

Then he lifted his head and looked at her face. Her
hair was scattered on the pillow and on her forehead;
Hiren lifted it and began to comb her soft hair gently
with his fingers. Only the outline of her face could be
seen in the dark; the darkness of her eyes and
eyebrows; her nose; the delicate line of her lips.

'Sheila, scared of what?' he asked.

'I don't know. It's so quiet here, and the relentless sound of the waterfalls woke me up. I couldn't sleep, Hiren! . . . our . . . our love—how will it turn out?'

'Turn out? Our love?' He remained silent for a moment and then continued, 'Listen to me, Sheila, my love! When I was talking to you about my country today, I only mentioned the bitter realities there. There's another aspect to the picture too. There are many good things there as well. In the evening, the sun goes down during the monsoon and the sky catches fire, and the moon emerges and the river flowing between the colourful fields of my country and its flourishing plains becomes a trembling, resplendent line of molten silver; and this country's millions of hardworking people, who wish to break open the chains of their poverty and slavery—they are all precious. This picture, its beauty filled with so much passion and gentleness, I, too, wish to enter it somehow. The desire to be part of this beauty, the struggle to partake of it—this, to me, is what life is. This is what it means to be alive . . .

'There's no other way of life for us. The other paths lead us to the dry, sandy desert of spiritual death and leave us stranded—from where there's no way out.

'Both of us will walk together on this path of life, which isn't easy, but is still filled with those joys, the rewards of life's struggle.

'My love! Our love itself should be an example of these joys, and if this doesn't happen, it will become a lamp which uses up its oil and is overpowered by the darkness of night. But, Sheila, we won't let it die out! We'll keep this lamp aflame with the sweat of our combined efforts.'

'And if the unmerciful hand of time separates us? If the gods of race, nation, state and community mercilessly stop us from reaching out to each other, and alienation and distance become shackles for our feet—then? What will we do, then?' asked Sheila.

'Don't frighten me, Sheila! I don't have the answers to your questions, except that one must struggle and hope. Behind everything that is possible, there lurks the frightful face of impossibility. If we give the prospect of impossibility room in our minds, our present life and the one to come will become tasteless and unbearable.'

'Hiren, my precious Hiren. My love!' Her voice was cracking; two streaks of tears had streamed down from the corner of her eyes. 'Forgive me. I don't know anything. I don't understand a thing apart from the fact that I love you very, very much.'

'And, Sheila, I too love you very, very much as well,' Hiren replied softly.

They embraced each other and in the midst of the entire world's struggles, troubles, wars and conflicts, their ears heard only one sound—that of each other's beating hearts.

Sheila finished her cigarette. She threw the butt in the fireplace and rose from her chair.

'It's been a year and a half since he returned to India, Naim. And I haven't heard from him in six months; there are no replies to my letters. He's from Bengal, where the youth who want freedom don't stay free for long. I'm worried. Could he have been arrested? No! My Hiren could never be a criminal!' Sheila asserted in a loud voice.

Naim replied, 'You don't have to be a criminal to be imprisoned in India; the desire for freedom is enough! But, Sheila, don't give up hope. Since he loves you so much, he'll certainly write to you. It must be something small that has kept him from it.'

Sheila smiled sorrowfully. 'Thanks for your consolation, Naim!' She went towards the window and looked out. From one corner of the sky, light had stirred and ripped through the curtains of darkness.

'Oh dear, it's morning now. Forgive me for sitting here and talking for so long. But, Naim, I was helpless. You understand, don't you? All right, I should go now.'

She quickly put on her coat and hat and, shaking Naim's hand, hurried towards the door. Naim followed her.

'Will we ever meet again?' he asked.

'I don't know. Goodbye, Naim!' Saying this, she slowly opened the door and left.

Naim quietly returned to his easy chair, sat down and stayed there, motionless, for a long time. The fire went out. The room fell cold. The faint gleam of morning, like a thief on tiptoe, began to steal in through the window.

P.S.

Insights
Interviews &
More . . .

Sajjad Zaheer Ke Naam

Faiz Ahmed Faiz

Na ab hum saath sair-e-gul karenge
Na ab mil kar sar-e-maqtal chalenge
Hadis-e-dilruban baham karenge
Na khoon-e-dil se shar'h-e-gham karenge
Na laila-e-sukhan ki dostdaari
Na ghamha-e-watan par ashkbari
Sunenge naghma-e-zanjir mil kar
Na shab bhar mil ke chhalkaenge saghar
Banaam-e-shaahid-e-naazuk khayalan
Bayaad-e-masti-e-chasm-e-ghazalan
Banaam-e-imbisaat-e-bazm-e-rindaan
Bayaad-e-kulfat-e-ayyaam-e-zindaan

Saba aur uska andaz-e-takallum
Sahar aur uska aghaz-e-tabassum
Fiza men ek hala sa jahan hai
Yehi to masnad-e-pir-e-mughan hai
Sahargaih ab usi ke nam saqi
Karen itmam-e-dawr-e-jam saqi
Bisat-e-bada-o-mina utha lo
Barha do sham-e-maih'hil, bazm walo
Piyo ab ek jam-e-alwida'i
Piyo, aur pike saghar tor dalo

Delhi, September 1973

A Requiem

Translated by Qurratulain Hyder

We'll roam no more in the valley of roses
Nor sit side by side under the shade of the gallows,
Gloomy twilights will not catch us in our frenzied search in the Desert,
Nor shall we stroll in the sunshine along boulevards of lovely women.
We'll talk no more of those we loved—the ravishers of hearts,
Nor write of our agony with our blood.

We'll befriend no more the Laila of Verse and Song
We'll mourn no more for our unhappy land,
Nor hear the clanking of the gaoler's chains.
We'll fill no more crystal cups
And drink all night to the Muse of thought,
Or to the memory of the gazelle-eyed, to joyful camaraderie,
Nor to the grimness of prison days.
Behold the halo in the empty space: the Wise Man of the Tavern
is gone.

O Saqi, to him let's pledge this dawn.
We shall drink the last round, O friends,
Blow out the candle and bid adieu,
Drink up your liquor and smash the cups.

Translator's Afterword

Bilal Hashmi

... one of the 'three slender paperbacks' (as Ali Sardar Jafri has fondly described them) with which the Progressive Writers' Association made its entry on the Indian literary scene.

A *Night in London* was first published from Lucknow in 1938, one of the 'three slender paperbacks' (as Ali Sardar Jafri has fondly described them) with which the Progressive Writers' Association made its entry on the Indian literary scene. The novella, which has since run into several editions, occupies a singular position in the history of Urdu literature. There is nothing quite like it, so far as I know, in Indian writing of roughly the same period, and that alone would seem to provide impetus enough for the work's belated translation into English.

Still, a few words are in order here, a translator's apology, if you will, as to the limits and intention of the present undertaking. Ever the consummate strategist, Zaheer chose Urdu as the language for this, his most important literary labour. In doing so he parted company with Mulk Raj Anand, Raja Rao and other expatriate contemporaries writing in European languages, largely on the grounds that a new Indian literature could only take shape from within the indigenous literary traditions of India. It was doubtless a political decision at the time (as it remains today), and one which kept the work at a remove from the same world literary marketplace into which it now stands the risk of being all but subsumed.

There is, in spite of all this, a very poignant sense that *A Night in London* was always already immersed in the 'world republic of letters' but never quite of it. Zaheer's novella was written with as much a nod to the 'socialist realist' Aragon of *Le Monde réel* (with whom the author rubbed shoulders in Paris), as to English literature's canonical modernists, Joyce and Woolf. It is widely regarded as the first major work of Urdu literature to employ the stream-of-consciousness technique, and that too with an expressly anti-colonial slant, far more radical, at least in that one respect, than anything that had until then emerged from within the Bloomsbury circle. Back home in Lucknow, it could lay claim to being the most innovative thing in Urdu prose since the novelistic experiments of Sarshar, Sharar and Ruswa in the nineteenth century.

For all its stylistic experimentation, *A Night in London* was framed by its author as a narrative of return (London-Paris-Lucknow), an ambivalent homage to European life. The novella partakes of a distancing strategy, but it is nonetheless marked by a certain tension, one that has proved more difficult to translate than anything else. Zaheer was a committed

> It is widely regarded as the first major work of Urdu literature to employ the stream-of-consciousness technique, and that too with an expressly anti-colonial slant, far more radical, at least in that one respect, than anything that had until then emerged from within the Bloomsbury circle.

realist, and yet with this work he was on the verge of creating, in tandem with other non-European writers of his generation, something radically new—a modernism against modernism.

In translating *A Night in London*, I have tried to preserve some of the foreignness of the original, while keeping it more or less 'fluent', and that principally because it struck me as the most effective way of grappling with the many challenges presented by a work born of such conflicting impulses. It might also be the real impetus for rendering the novella into a European tongue now, after all these decades: not to expand the canon of modernism, but to rethink the thing itself. To this end, an effort has been made to preserve certain idiomatic expressions and to retain, wherever possible, the intricacies of sentence structure in Urdu. I leave it to the reader to judge the results.

[H]is real creative achievement is the unfolding of the finest talent in the subcontinent, for he inspired hundreds of new writers.

—Ali Sardar Jafri

About the Author and His Works

Carlo Coppola

Syed Sajjad Zaheer (1905–1973) is one of the most important figures in twentieth-century Urdu and South Asian literature. Yet, his output of creative, belletristic writing—fiction, drama and poetry—is relatively slim as compared to other writers of comparable rank and stature. This portion of his oeuvre consists of a group of five short stories which appeared in *Angare* (1932), a ground-breaking and controversial collection of works by him and three other writers: Ahmed Ali (1910–1994), Rashid Jahan (1905–1952), and Mahmuduzzafar (1908–1956). Besides the five stories that featured in *Angare*, Zaheer's creative output is made up of a one-act play, *Bimar* (1936); the novella *Landan ki ek rat* (1938), the focus of this essay and the translation of which—*A Night in London*— is presented here; and a volume of prose poems, *Pighla nilam* (1964), which received respectful critical notice.

More than anything else Sajjad Zaheer is remembered in the Indian subcontinent for the new direction he gave to [. . .] writing in the turbulent times when the country was locked in a life-and-death struggle with a mighty colonial power.

—Kartar Singh Duggal

However, his expository writings, in comparison, are wide-ranging and varied: a major critical study of the poet Hafiz, *Zikr-i-hafiz* (1954), scores, if not hundreds, of editorial pieces for various journals of which he was the editor or to which he was a regular contributor, critical essays, political tracts, book reviews, journalistic pieces, reportage, memoirs, and Urdu translations of works by Shakespeare (*Othello*), Voltaire (*Candide*), Tagore (*Gora*), and Gibran (*The Prophet*).

His most important work of non-fiction is *Roshnai* or possibly *Rushnai* (1956), a personal reminiscence and chronicle of the beginnings, rise, and the start of the etiolation of the Progressive Movement in Urdu literature from 1936 to about the middle of 1947. An English translation of this work by Amina Azfar has been published as *The Light: A History of the Movement for Progressive Literature in the Indo–Pak Subcontinent* by Oxford University Press, in 2006. Completed while Zaheer, who was sent to Pakistan by the Communist Party of India to found its Pakistan wing, was imprisoned there from 1951 to 1954 due to his alleged link with the infamous Rawalpindi Conspiracy Case, *Roshnai*, written from a distinctive point of view, is one of the major sources for the study of this movement, which held a powerful sway over Urdu literature, and other Indian literatures as well, from the mid-1930s to the 1950s. His contribution to Urdu literature was recognized by the Sahitya Akademi—India's

... Zaheer, who was sent to Pakistan by the Communist Party of India to found its Pakistan wing, was imprisoned there from 1951 to 1954 due to his alleged link with the infamous Rawalpindi Conspiracy Case ...

national academy of letters—which celebrated the centenary of his birth with a two-day seminar held in New Delhi on 17–18 December 2005. The celebration was accompanied by the release of the monograph *Sajjad zaheer: hayat aur adabi khidmat* (Sajjad Zaheer: Life and Literary Achievements) by the distinguished Urdu literary critic Qamar Rais in its 'Makers of Indian Literature' series. (Incidentally, it is curious that an English-language version of this work about such an important Indian writer has not been published for wider distribution in the world of letters beyond Urdu readers; perhaps one is eventually planned.) Other festivities and celebrations to commemorate this occasion were held elsewhere in India and in Pakistan.

Scholars and critics generally refer to the 1932 publication of *Angare* as the starting point of the Progressive Movement in Urdu, and, by extension, in all South Asian literatures. The manner in which the volume came into being was happenstance.

In the middle of 1931, twenty-six-year-old Zaheer returned from England, where he had just received his B.A. (Honours) degree from Oxford University. While there, he was associated with left-wing and radical elements in both the Indian and the larger student bodies. In Mussoorie, he met Ahmed Ali, a twenty-one-year-old who stood 'first-class first' in the English B.A. (Honours) and M.A. programmes at Lucknow University with the highest marks received by any student till that time and for many

Scholars and critics generally refer to the 1932 publication of *Angare* as the starting point of the Progressive Movement in Urdu, and by extension, in all South Asian literatures.

years thereafter. The two men were similar in many respects: both were young, brilliant, single, educated through the medium of English, and shared a fondness, according to Ahmed Ali, for 'sombreros, bright shirts and contrasting ties, collecting candlesticks and gargoyles, Bach and Beethoven, and an admiration for James Joyce and D.H. Lawrence, and the *New Writing* poets, as well as Chekhov and Gorky'.

But there were stark differences too. Zaheer came from an upper-class Shia zamindari family, with his father Sir Syed Wazir Hasan being the distinguished chief justice of the Royal Court of Awadh in Allahabad. Though Ali's forefathers, ulema, had originally been invited to India from Persia by Emperor Shahjahan, they lost their privileged status after 1857. So, Ali's immediate family's circumstances were considerably humbler than Zaheer's. Ali's father was a middle-level civil servant who passed away when Ali was young, about eight or nine. By custom, then, Ali's mother and the family were required to live in the home of a paternal uncle, who was, in this instance, zealously orthodox. His wife was a woman whom Ali described as stingy and mean-spirited. Both also scorned the young man's interest in English and western education.

But a feature which cinched the relationship between these young men was that both had been writing fiction. In fact, Ahmed Ali had already published two short stories, one in English and the other in

Urdu. They were soon joined by two mutual friends: the smart, beautiful, witty and outspoken gynaecologist working at Lady Dufferin Hospital, Lucknow, Rashid Jahan, who was the daughter of one of the champions of women's education, Shaikh Muhammad Abdullah; and Mahmuduzzafar, the handsome son of Sahabzada Saiduzzafar Khan, head of the Medical College of Lucknow University and a prominent member of the ruling Rohilla Pathan family of Rampur. Schooled almost entirely in English, including Sherbourne School, Dorset, and Oxford University, Mahmuduzzafar refused to appear for the Indian Civil Service exam and had taken to wearing handloom cloth in support of Gandhi's boycott of British goods. In a personal correspondence to me from Karachi dated 16 August 1972, Ahmed Ali stated that since even the combined number of Zaheer's and his stories was not sufficient to publish as an anthology, the four friends 'decided on an evening to write a story each within a day' to bring the number of items up to a publishable level.

The collection, whose full title is *Angare: das mukhtasar kahanion ka majmua* (Embers: A Collection of Ten Short Stories), was published either late in 1931, possibly December, or early 1932, the latter date being the one most often cited. As the title indicates, it consists of ten works: five short stories by Zaheer, two by Ahmed Ali, and one by Mahmuduzzafar; and a short story and a one-act play by Rashid Jahan. This one-act play is often mistakenly called a short story by uninformed critics and scholars who have relied only on the book's subtitle for a description of its contents (truth to tell, the volume was, for many years, nearly impossible to secure). An analysis of these early works by Zaheer shows a number of literary features and socio-political concerns which he also addressed in *A Night in London*: India's nationalist aspirations, the plight of India's lower classes, Marxist economics, a disdain for organized religion (especially Islam) and for India's elite feudal classes, Freudian interpretations of human sexuality, and experimentation with a number of then-fashionable literary techniques such as fragmentary, fleeting thoughts, leaps in syntax and punctuation, complex flashbacks and flashbacks within flashbacks, ambiguous speaker identification, monologues, and stream-of-consciousness.

> An analysis of these early works by Zaheer shows a number of literary features and socio-political concerns which he also addressed in *A Night in London* ...

In Zaheer's works, for example, we meet such characters as the head-strong, exploited servant girl Dulari; the dishonest, sexually repressed Maulana Daud; the obsequious, morally compromised Munshi Barkat Ali; and others who are nameless. Each of these carefully drawn characters permits Zaheer to make his steely, honest gaze fall upon Indian society and reveal his uncompromising, empathetic view of the plight of India's underclasses and the callow insensitivity of its elites.

I have discussed the scandal surrounding the publication of *Angare* elsewhere. Briefly, the extreme reactions to the book were a result of hearsay, for it was not widely distributed (only about 200 copies were printed), nor is it likely to have been read by those who decried it. Newspapers and religious groups condemned it; public burnings of the book were held, and threats were made against the authors' lives. By March 1933, the book was officially banned by the United Provinces authorities under Section 295A of the Indian Penal Code for offending the sensibilities of a religious community.

Shortly after its proscription, a defence of the book, written by Ahmed Ali and Mahmuduzzfar, was published in the letters-to-the-editor section of the *Leader* (Allahabad) on 5 April 1933. A significant feature of this lengthy, forcefully argued editorial piece is the call for the formation of a 'League of Progressive authors' from the various languages of India to support the kind of political, social, and literary reforms implied in *Angare*.

In the meantime, Sajjad Zaheer was whisked off to Europe by his parents, first to Switzerland, a visit which probably allowed him to write so exactingly about the mountainous scenery in *A Night in London*, and then to London to study law. There he continued his affiliation with leftist Indian students at Oxbridge and the University of London, most notable among whom was the budding novelist Mulk Raj Anand (1905–

... Zaheer was whisked off to Europe by his parents, first to Switzerland, a visit which probably allowed him to write so exactingly about the mountainous scenery in *A Night in London*, and then to London to study law.

2004). Together they formed the Indian Progressive Writers' Association, which held its first meeting in the back-room of the Nanking Restaurant in Bloomsbury, very likely on the evening of 24 November 1934. This London group developed a manifesto which went through various iterations and espoused broad, humanistic, leftward-leaning sentiments: the importance of literature in a free, democratic society, the responsibility of writers to challenge reactionary and retrograde forces in society, the role of writers in shaping the social and political fabric of a nation, the need for support—both moral and financial—for writers, etc. These concepts were being expressed among writers and intellectuals internationally too. The manifesto was eventually published in both India (in a Hindi translation) and in Great Britain.

This was, of course, the period of the rise of fascism in Germany, Italy and Japan, and of the fear of its breaking out in Spain. To focus world attention on these ominous signs, a group of major French writers—André Gide (1869–1951), Henri Barbusse (1873–1935), Romain Rolland (1866–1944) and André Malraux (1901–1976)—organized the Soviet-sponsored International Congress for the Defence of Culture in Paris on 21–25 June 1935. Its intent was to promote and coordinate solidarity among writers around the world against the fascist threat. The list of speakers and attendees at this congress included writers from over fifteen countries, some of them the most eminent writers of

... the Indian Progressive Writers' Association, [. . .] held its first meeting in the back-room of the Nanking Restaurant in Bloomsbury, very likely on the evening of 24 November 1934.

the day: Forster, Huxley, Ehrenburg, Mann and Pasternak, in addition to the organizers, just to name a few. Among the 4000 or so audience members were two young virtual unknowns: Sajjad Zaheer and Mulk Raj Anand.

Several British and French writers, especially Ralph Fox (1900–1936) and Louis Aragon (1897–1982), encouraged Zaheer and Anand in their efforts to mobilize writers in India for the same purpose. Aided by his *Angare* colleagues, Zaheer began laying the groundwork for the establishment of a left-leaning, anti-fascist writers' association in India, not unlike the 'League of Progressive authors' called for in the 1933 defence of *Angare* in the *Leader*. He sailed home in November 1935. During this trip, he was finishing his novella, and, reaching India, he visited various major literary, intellectual, and political figures—Tagore, Nehru, and Gandhi himself among them—seeking and receiving support for the Progressives' efforts. Zaheer and Anand's labours bore fruit. The group held its first meeting in Lucknow on 9–10 April 1936, with the doyen of Hindi literature, Munshi Premchand (1880–1936), delivering the major address. The manifesto of this meeting, based on the earlier one written in London, explicitly called for reform in various aspects of India's literary, political, social, and religious life and established a formal entity, the All-India Progressive Writers Association. This organization was to become a major driving force in India's intellectual life and was to heavily influence

Aided by his *Angare* colleagues, Zaheer began laying the groundwork for the establishment of a left-leaning, anti-fascist writers' association in India, not unlike the 'League of Progressive authors' called for in the 1933 defence of *Angare* in the *Leader*.

various Indian literatures, especially Urdu, for the next two decades.

The dominant figure in this association was Sajjad Zaheer.

—

The dominant figure [in the PWA] was Sajjad Zaheer.

Sajjad Zaheer tells us in his laconic yet significant foreword to *A Night in London*, dated 15 September 1938, that the novella was authored while he was living in London and Paris, and when he was on board a ship while returning from Europe over two years earlier—probably mid- to late-1935–1936. He describes this period as his being 'under the spell of private emotional conflict'. It is difficult to determine exactly what he was referring to. He might have had in mind, for example, the regret he likely felt when Rashid Jahan—from whom he had secured a promise of marriage prior to leaving for England in the wake of the *Angare* scandal, and whom he had left in Mahmuduzzafar's 'care'—married Mahmuduzzafar in 1934. Then again, it might refer to some other unsuccessful emotional attachment he may have developed in Switzerland or England in the interim, or which he relinquished in order to pursue his political commitments (think Hiren Pal in *A Night in London*). Or, yet again, the distress may not have had anything to do with his love life at all. It could even refer to something more abstract or philosophical; for example, his coming to terms with the realization that his desire to be a purely creative writer was a pipe dream and that his future as a man of letters lay in other kinds and different areas of literary endeavour: journalism, polemics, translation, editing, organizing, etc. Whatever the conflict or conflicts may have been, he seems to have resolved them by the later months of 1938, for he indicates that his 'taking part in the revolutionary movement of workers and peasants in India, breathing in unison with millions of people and listening to the beating of their hearts' had been more important than writing *A Night in London*.

Then again, perhaps the resolution of these conflicts might have come about because, three months after writing the foreword, he married twenty-one-year-old Razia Dilshad, subsequently known as Razia Sajjad Zaheer. The literarily inclined, purdah-observing daughter of the principal of Ajmer Islamia High School, she shared many of Zaheer's views on politics, society and religion. Due to her considerable talent and vital creativity—together with Zaheer's support and encouragement, often expressed in eloquent, highly personal letters he wrote during their many separations due to his extensive travels and several imprisonments—as well as a need to generate income during Zaheer's frequent absences, she eventually become a prolific, highly successful creative writer of Urdu fiction. Perhaps his forthcoming wedding, as well as his interaction with workers and peasants, prompted him to state in the foreword: 'Today I could not write a book of this kind'; and to conclude, somewhat enigmatically: 'nor do I consider it necessary to write it'. The logical question to ask after reading this last remark is: was it necessary to publish it, then?

There are any number of reasons why Sajjad Zaheer may have decided to publish this work, in spite of what might strike some readers of the foreword as not-too-subtle ambivalence about seeing it in print. The most obvious reason may be found in the opening line of his foreword: learning about the lives of Indian students living in London during this period. This alone is perhaps the best reason for seeing it in print and translated here. Similar accounts have been written by Indians about their experiences as students in England, perhaps the most famous ones being by M. K. Gandhi and Jawaharlal Nehru. However, unlike the works by Gandhi and Nehru, Zaheer presents a richly textured, tightly organized, fictionalized glimpse into the lives of a diverse group of Indian students, Muslim and Hindu, from various parts of India and from several social strata, from middle-class to royalty. None, however, is from the worker or peasant classes to whom Zaheer alludes in his foreword. These English-speaking, educated elites are shown interacting among themselves and with English men and women in a brief, perhaps fourteen-hour, period from 6:00 p.m. on a November evening till sun-up (about 8:00 a.m.) the next morning, engaging in many activities, including talking, waiting about, drinking, smoking, dancing, 'spacing out', flirting, planning seductions,

Zaheer presents a richly textured, tightly organized, fictionalized glimpse into the lives of a diverse group of Indian students ...

dreaming, bragging, joking, teasing, reminiscing, and thinking. Many of these activities are not found in either Gandhi's or Nehru's accounts.

Several of the characters in this novella are vividly drawn. In the first few pages of the work, we are introduced to the angry, love-sick Azam, whose romantic involvement with the English girl Jean causes him much heartache, confusion, and anxiety. He is reluctant to return to India where his mother, as he learns in a letter from his younger sister, has 'picked out a nice bride' for him. He wants to stay in England and, presumably, marry Jean, for she is hardly the kind of woman—girl, actually—who would fare well in India. Such a match has disaster written all over it, whether in England or India.

Several of the characters in this novella are vividly drawn.

Azam's friend Rao, who is very successful with the ladies, is an outspoken, quick-witted cynic, a law student from Madras. A realist about life in India, especially regarding the debilitating effects of British domination and the destructive nature of communal politics, he cannot extricate himself from his negative thinking about everyone—Indians and British—and everything, especially politics. He is also sceptical about his prospects in India, even about his relationships with women. Nevertheless, experienced in matters of the heart, he offers Azam sympathy and words of caution in the latter's dealings with Jean. Rao is overwhelmed by an almost debilitating sense of powerlessness: the feeling of an inability to act or do anything in the face of forces which seem to be sweeping him and everyone around him towards some sort of large-scale disaster. Could this feeling have been Zaheer's foreboding about the Second World War?

The tall, robust Punjabi, Ahsan, the son of an Indian civil servant, stands in stark contrast to Rao. While Ahsan shares many of Rao's thoughts and opinions, he believes that he is perfectly capable of confronting the myriad problems which seem to overwhelm Rao. He does so with conviction and without doubts. He proposes action on 'revolutionary principles'. Clearly a Marxist, he is even called a Bolshevik by the aristocratic Khan Sahib. Talking with Rao as they head home after a party early in the morning, Ahsan elaborates upon his thinking and his plan of action for workers and labourers. His sentiments are reflected in Zaheer's foreword in his statement about working on behalf of the workers and peasants of India. Given the trajectory that Zaheer's life takes as a political writer and organizer, it would seem that, in his thinking and in his call to action, Ahsan is Zaheer's alter ego. Significantly, it is Ahsan who out-thinks and out-talks the brilliant, argumentative Rao, who quietly admits to a 'strange sort of mental apathy' that envelops him and renders him incapable of acting, a sad admission that he would probably make to no one else.

Hiren Pal—a Bengali medical student who is in a relationship with one of the central characters named Sheila—is also

... it would seem that [. . .] Ahsan is Zaheer's alter ego.

capable of action. He is presented to us through Sheila's love-biased eyes and words in her long monologue which occupies most of the novella's last chapter. Handsome, articulate, witty, and playful, Hiren intends to dedicate himself to the uplift of the Indian people through his work as a doctor. He indicates that if Sheila wants to be in his life, she must be willing to be part of his work and dedication. She agrees. He went back to India a year and a half ago, Sheila confesses to Naim, the host of the party, whom she has met just hours before, admitting both sadness and disappointment, which are perhaps tinged with hopelessness. She has not heard from him in the last six months. The reader is left to speculate what will happen to this relationship.

Naim is, in many respects, the most fully drawn and sympathetic male character in the novella.

Naim is, in many respects, the most fully drawn and sympathetic male character in the novella. A student of history, he is fat and jolly (at least on the outside), self-effacing and unsure of himself, and suffers from a severe case of *thesis interruptus chronicus*, a condition doubtless found in all graduate schools worldwide. Yet, everyone loves Naim. He is the nodal point that connects all the characters, both Indian and English. It is in his rented room that the party, the venue for most of the action of the novella, takes place. He is charmingly awkward as he tries to woo the golden-haired Sheila, who senses his innate goodness and trustworthiness. As a result, she opens up to him when everyone else has left after the party, and relates the story of her meeting and involvement with

Hiren Pal, thus dashing any ideas Naim might have had of a romantic relationship with her. He also shows tact and understanding as he attempts to tamp down the drunken talk and antics of boisterous, unruly guests. He is witty and humorous as he tries to temper the priggishness of the only female Indian character in this work, Karima Begum, with jokes and flattery. However, in his thoughts, he castigates her for her hauteur and surliness.

Karima does not come off very well here. She is clearly a woman caught in the crosshairs of tradition and modernity. She is traditional in many ways: attitudes, conversation, opinions and sartorial sense. Yet, she is strikingly modern in her pursuit of a graduate degree in spite of opposition from her family. Obviously highly intelligent, she boasts that she has reached England on her own—having been awarded a full scholarship for her studies—rather than depending on financial support from her family, which all the others seem to have. But she is capable of pettiness and jealousy. For example, she refuses to dance at the party because it's what prostitutes and actresses do in India. She also admonishes the men for losing their good Indian manners and adopting what she considers rude British ways. And in an interior monologue, she viciously attacks Sheila, of whom she is jealous because the English girl has replaced her as the centre of the men's attention. Karima enjoys that position, yet, when there, sends the men mixed signals. When they approach, she reproaches. A classic case of approach-avoidance, indecision and insecurity.

Karima arrives at the party with another student, Arif, a self-absorbed, politically conservative snob from a wealthy family, who is obsessed with passing the Indian Civil Service exam, which he had, in fact, failed when he took it previously in India. He and his family believe that he will fare better by appearing for the exam in England. He rationalizes that his failure in India was not due to his own shortcomings but because of the prejudice of Hindu examiners. He lives in an exclusive part of the city, wears expensive clothes, and has developed a plummy British accent. An avid reader of *The Times*, he even commits sentences from it to memory, intending to use them later, without attribution, in his ICS exam. He envisions himself as a high-level magistrate lording it over masses of Indians and becomes peevish when accused of wishing to preserve the malignant status quo between Great Britain and India. He is further upset when he tries, unsuccessfully, to gain Sheila's full attention and eventually leaves the party with an unnamed actress, a free spirit who is underwhelmed by his declarations of self-importance. He assumes that since she is an actress and, therefore, sexually liberated, he can lure her to his room for the night. Instead, he cuts a pathetic figure as she abandons him after buying a newspaper, not *The Times* but the *Daily Worker*—certainly a blow to Arif's ego and self-esteem, not to mention his conservatism—and jumps on a bus to go home by herself, thus destroying his hopes of bedding her.

Two minor characters, Singh and Khan Sahib, are from India's upper classes. The drunken, outspoken Singh is a braggart, a Chandarbansi Rajput, whose distinguished kshatriya or warrior lineage goes back to Lord Krishna himself, making Singh 'a descendant of the moon'. He compares his ancestral pedigree with that of his companion, Khan Sahib, a bona fide prince, a shahzada who, in turn, brags that he is 'a nobleman'. The latter's Pathan ancestors were originally from Bokhara and were brought to India by Emperor Akbar. Khan is attracted to Jean, Azam's girlfriend, but she quickly dismisses him. In several ways, this character's background resembles that of Mahmuduzzafar, a Rohilla Pathan and a member of the extended family of the royal house of Rampur, who, according to his younger sister, the late Dr Hamida Saiduzzafar, was often addressed—at times seriously and humorously on other occasions—by many (including his charismatic wife, who would, often and teasingly, engage him and anyone else in playful badinage) as sahibzada, roughly, 'prince'. This character is perhaps Zaheer's bit of sweet revenge against Mahmuduzzafar vis-à-vis Rashid Jahan. Even if this were so, it must be said that elsewhere in his writings, notably in *Roshnai*, Zaheer portrays Mahmuduzzafar with considerable respect, genuine admiration, and comradely warmth.

[Khan Sahib] is perhaps Zaheer's bit of sweet revenge against Mahmuduzzafar vis-à-vis Rashid Jahan.

Moreover, given the subsequent close cooperation among the three of them in organizing the All-India Progressive Writers' Association and numerous other undertakings on behalf of the Progressive Movement, it seems that all—or at least most—was forgiven.

Zaheer also presents the reader with a number of British characters. The first of these are Jim and Tom, two rough-hewn, shabbily dressed working-class men whom Rao and Azam meet in a pub. Jim asks Rao for a light and the two start talking. Jim expresses solidarity with striking Indian workers and insists that since the British have ruled India badly, they should withdraw and India should be free. He makes this point emphatically to his friend, Tom, who argues the time-worn, self-serving justification for continued British presence in India: the communal chaos and conflagration which would ensue if they left. Prescience about yet another future event?

Not all Brits are so friendly and respectful as Jim and Tom. Just as Azam and Rao are about to leave the pub, a sodden racist calls them 'blackies' and smarmily boasts of the good times he had in India during the war. Another such type is Naim's haughty landlady who calls him aside and demands that his guests leave because of their noisiness and the lateness of the hour.

Azam's girlfriend, Jean, is flighty, selfish, and superficial. She promises to meet him and fails to show up and then cajoles and teases him with sweet talk when he gets angry. Clearly enjoying the power she has over him, she is charming, coy, narcissistic and high maintenance; in other words, a 'tease', the very type of woman Azam does not need.

In contrast, Sheila Green, who expresses a profound love for India and a fascination with Indians, is highly articulate, observes carefully, listens well, speaks honestly, and is devoid of airs and pretensions. The sharp contrast between her and Jean is perhaps a bit facilely drawn. Nevertheless, she demonstrates a depth of character and personal warmth: traits that, among all the other characters in the novella, are shared only by Naim. She too is in love, but her lover, the idealist Hiren Pal, is now in India and has not communicated with her for over six months, leaving her with an uneasy feeling about his physical well-being, given the volatile political climate in India at the time. She fears that he may have gone to jail or has been injured somehow. A sad, unspoken possibility is, of course, that he is no longer interested in her. Her lengthy monologue in the seventh chapter relates the beginning and the growth of their relationship, and she narrates it with a palpable sense of place— the Swiss mountains—her elaborate descriptions of the milieu and trekking worthy of a poet. She is strong but vulnerable; and, like the other major characters in the story, she too is anxious and concerned about the future and what it holds for her.

In addition to these characters, Zaheer

has employed a number of literary features, some of which are also found in his *Angare* stories. Among these, interior monologues are the most revealing and frequent, often contrasting the character's unrestrained, frank, and often unkind thoughts with his or her tempered, often disingenuous, if not entirely dishonest, spoken words. The inherent grammatical feature of the Urdu language which allows third-person narrative to morph immediately into first-person direct quotes makes this device especially compelling.

Flashbacks are also used, several of them short and surrealistic, often induced by alcohol but also from drowsiness or just 'spacing out' for an instant. Sheila's lyrical flashback narrative is a highlight of the work. In some of the dialogue, the absence of speech tags requires the reader to pay close attention, or to risk losing track of who is saying what to whom, provoking intended ambiguity and confusion.

These features aside, there is no denying that the work contains shortcomings which detract from its purely literary quality. The most obvious is the author's undisguised didacticism. A harsh critic might concur that it diminishes the integrity of the narrative. One finds this tone in various extended statements made by Rao and Ahsan, for example. These read like speeches or lectures rather than the normal conversation between friends, especially in a party atmosphere. Moreover, such a critic would find an ally in an unnamed character at Naim's party who

. . . there is no denying that the work contains shortcomings which detract from its purely literary quality. The most obvious is the author's undisguised didacticism.

complains that Ahsan 'doesn't have any right to give a speech here. We've come here for a party, not to hear a lecture'. This remark suggests that Zaheer was well aware of this problem and was perhaps struggling with the dilemma it posed. In the end, didactic concerns seem to have trumped artistic ones.

But for another critic this might not be a problem. She could effectively argue that the didactic aspect of the work is one of its qualities, that Zaheer knew his Indian audience and felt the need to 'enlighten' them, for example, on something as seemingly trivial as how a pub is set up. He was aware that since most of his readers had not been to England, they would not know about the social arrangement and hierarchy of the place, and, by extension, its implications as a location in the story. Similarly, he was compelled to 'teach' his readers what he saw as the sterling qualities of Marxist–Leninist doctrine, about which they might know little or nothing. In any case, whatever position one might take on this question, most would agree that a lighter touch would have served the literary quality of this work positively.

A Night in London reveals Zaheer's personal struggle to use his art—literature, his creative writing—as an instrument of social change. Urdu has had a significant tradition of viewing literature as means of teaching and social uplift. However, as his foreword suggests, Zaheer seems to be well on his way to answering a different calling— one that was in the service of India's workers and peasants and which utilized his

A Night in London reveals Zaheer's personal struggle to use his art— literature, his creative writing— as an instrument of social change.

preternatural gift for organization. Something that his character Ahsan calls 'action'. This novella, then, is a sort of swansong for Sajjad Zaheer the creative writer, and his foreword to it a segue into the less rarefied, more rough-and-tumble realms of political organization, partisan journalism, and class struggle. The publication of *A Night in London*, then, added to his bona fides as a writer, a credential which would have supported his role as the liaison between the growing Communist Party of India and writers, not only in Urdu, but in all of the major literatures of India. This is a position which, for nearly two decades, made him one of the most powerful and commanding personas in twentieth-century South Asian letters and this novella a significant literary work in modern Urdu literature.

In conception and execution it is an entirely new thing in Urdu literature.
—Shaista Suhrawardy Ikramullah

Reminiscences

Sajjad Zaheer

Translated by Khalique Naqvi

> The truth was that before my eyes lay the panorama of Europe in particular and the world in general that was changing daily—the picture of a world dying and a new world being born.

Nineteen hundred and thirty five was a unique year. I was spending the last days of my student life in London. It was not really the life of a student, for the life which was to encircle me a few months later had already begun. I was staying in London to study law, which was now for me something of very little consequence. The truth was that before my eyes lay the panorama of Europe in particular and the world in general that was changing daily—the picture of a world dying and a new world being born. It was not because I was a young man of any exceptional understanding, or that my heart was made restless by the vision of an unhappy world. A large number of those in my midst, educated young men and women, Indians and English, were thinking on similar lines. It was the logical reaction to the stresses of the times.

Just remember the two years preceding

'35. The political effect of the economic crisis that engulfed the world took in Germany the shape of the dictatorship of Hitler and his Nazi Party. In London and Paris we daily came across miserable refugees who had escaped or were exiled from Germany. Everywhere one could hear painful stories of fascist repression. Ruffians in the service of capitalists were torturing freedom-loving people and communists in a thousand different ways. The ghastly picture of the beloved leaders of the people with the blue weals of whips on their backs and seats; the terrible acts of beheading of well-known communist leaders periodically published in the newspapers; the painful darkness which, spreading from the bright world of art and learning that was Germany, was throwing its fearful shadow on Europe—all this had shattered the inner tranquillity of our hearts and minds. Only one force could stem the tide of this modern barbarism—the organized power of factory workers, a power that had emerged from worker's solidarity, through cooperation, through ceaseless, everyday struggle against the repression and exploitation of capitalists. The experience of continuous class struggle had equipped this force with a revolutionary class consciousness, one that was enabling it to frustrate the attempts of a backward-looking capitalism and to become the architect of a new civilization.

Was it only a hope? A desire? The yearning of a traveller lost in darkness for just a dim ray of light that might pierce the terrible curtain of darkness?

Everywhere one could hear painful stories of fascist repression. [. . .] Only one force could stem the tide of this modern barbarism—the organized power of factory workers . . .

It was in Germany itself that the first ray of light emerged. To discredit the communists, Hitler and his henchmen—Goering, Goebbels, etc.—conspired to have the grand building of the Reichstag set on fire (March 1933) and got several communist leaders arrested on the plea that it was their doing. One of the accused was Dimitrov, a leader of the Communist Party of Bulgaria, who was living in exile in Berlin. When, after months spent in captivity, the hearing of the case against him opened, the eyes of the world were suddenly fixed on a room of the German court in Leipzig. The statements of Dimitrov not only proved him and his comrades innocent, but put the German fascists in the dock. And along with this he declared his uncompromising belief that fascism was not eternal in Germany, that one day the German workers would throw off the yoke of capitalism.

I remember quite well how, when the news of huge demonstrations of workers in America, England, France, etc., calling for the release of Dimitrov and his comrades came round, it forced even capitalist newspapers to admit the innocence of Dimitrov and to praise the courage with which he withstood the torture and threats of reprisals and continued to proclaim the truth before the court.

The unrest had now spread among the intellectuals as well. Many great writers of Germany (Thomas Mann, Toller, etc.), world-renowned scientists (Einstein, Haber, etc.), artists, musicians, doctors were already in exile and without any means of livelihood. Dimitrov's case and popular sympathy for the German exiles gradually brought into the camp of the anti-fascist movement, in one way or the other, a great number of intellectuals and writers from western Europe and America.

The general feeling was that if the fascist plague was not checked it would not remain confined to Germany but would spread its horrors to other countries of Europe. The conditions which had produced fascism were also developing fast in other countries. Even in so-called democracies, the capitalist class, which was till now exploiting the workers in the name of democracy, could easily throw off the garb, suppress civil liberties, destroy workers' organizations, wipe out all representative institutions and establish naked dictatorship.

The conditions which had produced fascism were also developing fast in other countries.

In the case of France, the danger was increasing daily. On the model of Germany, armed fascist gangs had started attacking the meetings and processions of workers. The government knew that behind these illegal activities were the owners of iron and coal mines and electric and steel factories, and the money-bags of financial magnates. It stood by and watched the increasing power of capitalists, the unlawful riots, but remained silent.

Then suddenly one day the news came that the French reactionaries had launched an offensive, that huge crowds had surrounded the Chamber of Deputies. The government had resigned out of fear, and a new cabinet had been formed which was more reactionary than the previous one. This event opened the eyes of everyone and the people started asking, 'Will this birthplace of liberty, equality and fraternity also resound, like Hitler's Germany, with the trumpet of fascism?'

The French working class soon gave a reply to this question. There was a glorious general strike, the communists raised the slogan of a 'Front Populaire', and, in spite of the reformist socialist leaders, there was a new solidarity among the trade unions. Every worker realized that becoming one with these powers could be decisive in a society dependent on machines. The general strike of workers in France gave strength to all freedom-loving people, and after this event signs of a new life emerged everywhere. The reactionary parties were being defeated and the working class's unity, discipline and power of action gradually drew the middle class towards it.

[Whilst this was taking place, a series of events transpired in Austria, which, although tragic, nonetheless carried a revolutionary splendour. The Treaty of Versailles had cut up Austria into a tiny state—the kind of state whose economic problems would prevent it from functioning unless it fell within the orbit of one or the other of Europe's large empires. Following the rise of Hitler and Mussolini, the French Empire's sway over Europe and the Balkans began to wane. Now both Italy and Germany were casting covetous glances upon Austria. The general economic crisis and conditions were also creating effects of their own. The democratic system which had been implemented in Austria after the Treaty of Versailles (that is, the system which garbs capitalism in the robes of democracy) was beginning to falter. So much so that one day the newspapers reported the annulment of the Austrian constitution. Parliament was dissolved indefinitely, all power snatched from the hands of the municipalities. A dwarfish man by the name of Dollfuss assumed for himself the reins of the Empire! That is to say, fascism seized upon another European nation. At the same time, or just a few days later, came another piece of news. Workers in Vienna, Linz and Graz—Austria's major industrial cities—had refused to accept the oppressive dictates of their usurping ruler; Dollfuss issued an order for the confiscation of all arms from workers' organizations; this led to a battle between government forces and the workers. The workers fought with great courage, managing to take possession of a number of strongholds in the city. Then came other news. The workers were being driven back on account of the government being better armed. And still they continued to fight with great bravery, even as they knew there now remained no hope for victory. A defeat in the end. But the bloody victory that the army had won, and the cruelties of its soldiers, lent credence to the strength of the working class.]

We began to feel that although fascism had prevailed on that day, on the other hand, the revolutionary consciousness of the toiling masses was increasing! The experience of this very failure would make possible a successful revolution!

Dimitrov's trial, the vigilance of the French workers, the unsuccessful workers' revolution in Austria—these events mean little to most people today, but for us they were of great significance. It was quite obvious that for a long time peace, tranquillity and ease had come to an end for humanity. We were witnessing all around us the commencement of a period of great international conflict and struggle. Would humanity ever be able to extricate itself from the flood of fire and steel? And was it possible for young men like us, in whose veins flowed the warm blood of life, to save ourselves from this storm? Our world of love, the charm of a well-formed beautiful body and eyes which captivate, conversation which we want to continue for ever, the beating of two hearts in unison—what would happen to all this? And that world of our dreams, a colourful world, scornfully colliding with conservatism, revolting against everything base, worshipping beauty, impatient to extract the bluish hue of the sky, the smell of flowers, the flow of water, in short, tapping into the essence of every bit of matter—how long would this dream world survive in this woebegone period? Was it possible for us to separate our private lives from the tumult and misery of society?

We were gradually drifting towards socialism. Our minds searched for a

We were witnessing all around us the commencement of a period of great international conflict and struggle.

philosophy which would help us to understand and solve difficult social problems. We were not satisfied with the idea that humanity had always been miserable and would always remain so. We read Marx and other socialist writers with great enthusiasm. As we proceeded with our studies, solved the historical, social and philosophical problems through mutual discussions, our minds became clear and our hearts contented. After the end of our university education, this was the beginning of a new and infinite field of education!

Most of the members of our small group wanted to become writers. And what else could they do? We were incapable of manual labour. We had not learnt any craft and our minds revolted against serving the imperialist government. What other calling was left? ['*You cannot become a kafir, and so, per force, you must become a Muslim.*' Mulk Raj Anand's *Untouchable* had already been published, and *Coolie* was on its way. Anand lived in a tiny room in Regent Square where he did his writing. It was either the case that we would all gather in his room, talk and drink tea, or, having broken it off with a sweetheart of his, he would divulge to us his tales of woe. Sometimes his voice would become faint, muffled; and at other times he would talk and laugh boisterously—a flame, bright, warm and quivering.

Dr Jyoti Ghosh would occasionally arrive from Oxford. His learning and acquirements inspired us with awe. He had obtained in English literature every single degree Oxford

We were not satisfied with the idea that humanity had always been miserable and would always remain so.

University had to offer. His two voluminous studies of an English poet of times past had just recently been published; and he had secured for himself, in England, a place among experts of the English language—a rather significant accomplishment for an Indian. In spite of all this, there was no ostentation in his manner. He was a lecturer in Bengali at Oxford and took great interest in Bengali literature. As a rule, he could not tolerate aesthetic shortcomings in literary works. He wished to see Indian literature free from spiritual (Vedantic) bonds, and was a fierce opponent of the purely contemplative stream in older poetry (in Hindi and Bengali)—that is, its excessive fixation with religious precepts.

It was Anand who introduced me to [Iqbal] Singh. At the time he had affected an amalgam of the styles of Lawrence and Joyce and was writing a novel in English. He lived in dire straits—God knows how he kept alive. His command of English was quite good. A socialist he was, perhaps, but one who stood firmly in opposition to Marxism. We thought of him as an idealist. But he himself would say that he did not wish to be associated with any system. At any rate, he was also someone with whom we engaged in much discussion. We all hoped that his book would be published before long, so that he, too, could attain a position in the ranks of writers. His novel soon came out, and subsequently he published a thick book on Gautama Buddha.]

Of a large number of Englishmen we used

to meet, Ralph Fox deserves a special mention. Though Fox was older than us by about ten years, he mixed with us so freely that all differences of nationality, age and language were obliterated and no one could surmise that he was a famous and recognized English author while we were only would-be writers.

One day I invited him to a dinner at my room to talk about the Progressive Writers' Association. A Bengali friend of mine cooked a dish which was something between *khichri* and *pulao*. Fox ate it with great relish. Till late he talked about his plan to visit India. In the course of the discussion regarding literature, he again and again warned us that our enthusiasm for progressivism must not degenerate into sectarianism and prejudice. When a Bengali friend of ours criticized Tagore for being a representative of India's capitalist class and a reactionary, Fox was upset. He characterized such talk as a caricature of Marxism. No poet or writer could be tied to any imaginary category so easily. This was the period when Fox was writing *Genghis Khan*. The memory of his grey hair, blue eyes, especially his bright informal laughter and then two years later his death in Spain as a soldier of freedom in the battlefield fighting against reactionary capitalism—this I will never forget. Never!

One day after consultation among ourselves a formal meeting was held in my room. There were no more than six or seven persons and a committee was constituted to organize the Indian Progressive Writers'

There were no more than six or seven persons and a committee was constituted to organize the Indian Progressive Writers' Association.

Association. In the beginning the work was slow, but soon all of us took greater interest. It was decided that a manifesto be drafted to formulate our aims and objectives. Four or five persons were commissioned to do the job. Anand prepared the first draft, which was very long. Later, this work was entrusted to Dr Ghosh who presented his draft before the committee. I was asked to rewrite the drafts of Anand and Ghosh (which we had discussed repeatedly for hours together) and prepare a final draft. After many disputes and long discussions about every sentence and every word, the committee finally approved the draft.

Very ceremoniously we held the first official meeting. During this period we had propagated a lot among Indians with literary leanings in London, Oxford and Cambridge. A Chinese restaurant owner of London was very considerate towards us and used to offer the back room of his restaurant free of charge. This small, unventilated cellar could accommodate forty to fifty people with difficulty. Our regular meeting was held there. Mulk Raj Anand was elected president and on behalf of the committee we presented the draft of the manifesto which was adopted after a few amendments. The four or five of us elected to the executive committee were very satisfied with the meeting. To collect about thirty to thirty-five Indians in London was in itself an achievement. Further, the drafting of the manifesto had helped to clarify scattered ideas. What is progressivism? What is the aim of progressive writers? How should

> It was decided that a manifesto be drafted to formulate our aims and objectives.

they work? The manifesto tried to answer these questions, however tentatively, which was an important achievement. When I find a discussion on these issues still raging in our magazines (in 1940)—which is, of course, a desirable thing—the comprehensiveness of our first manifesto becomes all the more apparent.

The meetings of the PWA (the name given to our organization) were now held once or twice a month in London. Once, a professor of Calcutta University, Dr Sumiti Kumar Chatterji, delivered a lecture before our Association in support of the Roman script. We believed in the Roman script ourselves, and his scientific lecture convinced us so thoroughly that we became strong supporters of the reform. The idea of one script for the entire country was very attractive, and in London the fire of prejudice and sentiments which blazes at the mention of this problem in India was completely absent. Hindi and Urdu-speaking people, Madrasis, Bengalis, Gujaratis—in short, young men from every part of India, were present there and all of them unanimously decided that the Progressive Writers' Association should propagate for the Roman script.

At another meeting a Bengali member read a paper in English on the poetry of Kazi Nazrul Islam, describing its revolutionary significance. Our custom was to discuss and criticize every article or story read before the meeting. In one of the later meetings Anand read his short story entitled

The idea of one script for the entire country was very attractive, and in London the fire of prejudice and sentiments which blazes at the mention of this problem in India was completely absent.

'The Terrorist' which was later published in *Asia*, an American magazine. I also read my Urdu one-act play, *Bimar*. After the stories published in the anthology *Angare*, this was my first work. There were few Urdu-knowing people in our Association, and hence the criticism of Dr Taseer (who was studying at Cambridge those days), Singh and Anand pleased me greatly. Yet I was feeling guilty. How ridiculous to imagine oneself to be a writer with only a few short stories and a small play to one's credit! The fame of *Angare* had reached the Indians in London. I was happy that my first literary effort had shocked the old, bearded fogeys. I was glad that Dr Abdul Haq's *Urdu* had praised my stories, though I had no illusions about my literary abilities! In this literary tumult, I began *A Night in London* to save my conscience.

We knew from the very beginning that living in London we could neither influence Indian literature nor create any good literature ourselves. Side by side with our realizing the advantages of forming the association in London, this feeling was strengthened. A few exiled Indians could do little more than draw up plans among themselves and produce an orphan-like literature under the influence of European culture. The most important thing that we learnt in Europe was that a progressive writers' movement could bear fruit only when it propagated in various languages and when the writers of India realize the necessity of the movement and put in practice its aims

... I began A Night in London to save my conscience.

and objectives. The best that the London Association could do was to put us in contact with the progressive literary movements abroad, to represent Indian literature in the West and to interpret for India the thoughts of Western writers and the social problems which were profoundly influencing Western literature.

Certain events which took place at that time in France helped us in our determination. I have already mentioned that the movement for a Popular Front against fascism in France had begun in 1933, and that the middle class was also being drawn towards it. Consistent efforts of the prominent French writer Henri Barbusse resulted in the calling of an 'International Congress of Writers for the Defence of Culture' in Paris in June, 1935. Sponsors of the conference included such famous personalities as Maxim Gorky, Romain Rolland, André Malraux, Thomas Mann and Waldo Frank. This meeting, held in the Mutualité, a famous hall of Paris, was of great historic significance for the literary world. It was the first occasion when the writers of almost every civilized nation had collected together at one place for consultation among themselves. For the first time they had felt the necessity of eschewing their individualism and organizing themselves to save civilization and culture from the rising tide of reaction and degeneration. This was the only way by which they could help the forces of progress, give full scope to the development and

The best that the London Association could do was to put us in contact with the progressive literary movements abroad, to represent Indian literature in the West and to interpret for India the thoughts of Western writers and the social problems which were profoundly influencing Western literature.

flowering of their creative abilities, and thus, in an organized manner, save themselves from annihilation in this revolutionary age.

It was to be expected that, at a conference so large, there would be writers of different beliefs and persuasions. On one issue, however, all were united. All believed that writers should, with every means in their power, defend the right of freedom of thought and opinion. Wherever fascist or imperialist forces attempt dictatorially to impose restrictions on writers or adopt repressive measures on account of their views, a powerful agitation should be launched against it.

The universal feeling at the conference was that the writers could defend themselves in the best possible manner by becoming a part of the People's 'United Front' for freedom and thus gaining the support of the labouring classes. The experience of the French and Chinese writers proved the truth behind this idea. At a time when China was engaged in mortal combat against Japanese imperialism, the best writers, poets, novelists, dramatists, educationists, philosophers and others were using all their talents for the success of their country in the war of liberation. The Chinese Writers' Association, an important part of the anti-imperialist united front, besides satisfying the literary needs of the Chinese people, also presented the most patent reality of Chinese life—the war against Japan—in its real colour to the people, thus preparing them psychologically for the war of liberation.

> **Wherever fascist or imperialist forces attempt dictatorially to impose restrictions on writers or adopt repressive measures on account of their views, a powerful agitation should be launched against it.**

In France, great philosophers, poets, novelists and other writers, under the leadership of Henri Barbusse, had built up an organization to fight against fascism. Undoubtedly, it was largely the indefatigable efforts and the general influence of these intellectuals which had brought the middle class into the united front movement of the proletariat and established a Popular Front which was ultimately successful in forming a government in the middle of 1936. Besides this, there was a separate association of socialist and communist writers which had its own monthly magazine.

The sessions of the international conference and meetings of its committees were held for several days. Thousands of people thronged the open sessions and the hall where the admission was by tickets and completely packed. One special feature was the presence of workers in large numbers, as if they were there to prove the newly established relationship between the writers and the people, to strengthen it, which was the special purpose of this conference. In the present-day capitalist society, writers as a group have been separated from the people, a little afraid of them, entertaining contempt for them in their hearts. In any case, they are unfamiliar with the people. The reason for the spiritual paralysis of a large part of modern literature lies in the distance that separates it from the source of life, the life of the labouring classes.

The delegation of Soviet writers at the conference was given a rousing reception

The reason for the spiritual paralysis of a large part of modern literature lies in the distance that separates it from the source of life, the life of the labouring classes.

because in the socialist society of the USSR there was no distance between the writer and his audience. The socialist writer belongs to the people and the people belong to him. Among these writers were the representatives of various nationalities like the Tatars, Uzbeks and Tajiks (the Tajik Soviet Socialist Republic lies in the north of Kashmir, where Persian is the language of the people).

It is regrettable that while Chinese, Japanese, Persians, Turks, Arabs, Tatars, and so on were adequately represented at the conference, Indian writers should have been represented by Ms Sophia Wadia, a Parsi lady from Bombay. It would have been better to leave India unrepresented rather than send her to represent the country! As for ourselves, few of us could labour under the misapprehension that we could represent the grand literature of India at the conference. Further, we were not authorized by any Indian literary organization to represent Indian writers there.

At the conclusion of the conference, an international centre of the progressive literary movement of the entire world was established in Paris. The members of this centre had already been elected at the conference. The progressive writers' movements in the various countries were being integrated not only intellectually but also organizationally. This was a big stride in the path of the creation of international culture. Our Progressive Writers' Association decided to get itself affiliated to this international literary centre. Later, when a Progressive Writers'

... an international centre of the progressive literary movement of the entire world was established in Paris.

Association would be formed in India we would maintain this affiliation as a foreign branch of the central organization in India, representing Indian literature in foreign countries according to the instructions of the parent organization.

During this period I had completed my law degree and was staying in Paris after giving up my residence in London. Here I lived with my friend Shaukatullah Ansari, who was studying medicine in Paris. Most of my time was spent writing *A Night in London*. I wanted to finish [the novella] before leaving for India, for I thought that once there I would not have time to complete this work.

[It was in the last days of winter that I arrived in Paris. The leaves on the trees of the wide pathways were a lush green. The river Seine was at its most beautiful. Along its banks were old bookstores and other second-hand shops, where people stood around sifting through books and could be seen strolling here and there, ever so casually. On the right bank of the river stands the cathedral of Notre Dame, its two rectangular towers appearing as though suspended from above; and from this elevation, the strange and frightening chimeras along the balustrades, those devilish caricatures, seem to be mocking the world of men below. Some two miles away, along the same bank, lies the Louvre Palace; and joined to it is the garden of the Tuileries. Every nook and corner of this district in Paris is historical, and within it are to be found the world's

During this period I [. . .] was staying in Paris [. . .] Most of my time was spent writing *A Night in London*. I wanted to finish [the novella] before leaving for India, for I thought that once there I would not have time to complete this work.

most splendid masterpieces of art. During the long summer evenings, the dark walls of the Louvre are surrounded by verdant trees, and, between the two wings of the Palace, are couched large, charming beds of autumnal flowers. At every corner are statues of famous French personalities, or else life-size sculptures of Greek gods and goddesses; a flowing stream of cars along the middle road. On the stone benches of the Tuileries sit young lovers in an embrace. A large pond with a wild, gushing fountain at its centre, at the edge of which children navigate a toy sail boat. The darkness of night was steadily enclosing upon us. From an elevated surface of the garden we glance towards the Place de la Concorde—a large square, which is surrounded by roads glistening with black coal tar. The conical, granite Obelisk of Luxor, decorated with ancient Egyptian hieroglyphics, is at the centre, and stands at the very place of the guillotine which, at the time of the French Revolution, severed the heads of Louis XVI, his Queen Marie Antoinette, and those of thousands of enemy nobles. All around it are ponds and fountains, and a cluster of bright lights, in the midst of which emerges that world-famous avenue, the Champs-Élysées, which means the 'heavenly fields', and whose wide expanse contains a jungle of trees lined along both sides. And at the opposite end of the avenue, in clear view of the Tuileries and some two miles away, is the Arc de Triomphe commissioned by Napoleon—tall, imposing, but also beautiful. The atmosphere, when observed from here, comes to life in the red glow of the setting sun. In spite of the steady stream of traffic, there is a measure of serenity at this time: the harmony of man and nature—a silent, pitiable joy. We cannot stay here long, for the Tuileries Garden closes at nightfall. From one of its corners, the caretaker is shouting whilst blowing a whistle, and the couples sitting in the park are reluctantly beginning to leave, hand in hand.]

This was the city Parisians called the 'Queen of the World', and which I was witnessing perhaps for the last time. These were the days when the lamp of our newly awakened hopes glowed brightly because of the movement for a united front of the workers and people of France. We felt that the glow of this spark would gradually increase and that its flame would spread to other countries in Europe. Slowly the fire of revolution would blaze everywhere, creating a new world, a new sky, a new earth and in fact a new Man. We knew that our path would be difficult but in that refreshing warmth of spring we had no idea that it would be as tortuous as it turned out to be after the beginning of the Second World War!

I considered my stay at the centre of the new literary movement to be useful for my intellectual development. Unfortunately, a few days after the international conference, Barbusse died, and I could not meet him. Many years earlier I had heard him speak, though I did not get an opportunity to talk

... [Zaheer] was not at all aware that [. . .] **A Night in London** *[holds] a unique place in literature . . .*
—Ismat Chughtai

to him. His funeral procession was attended by hundreds of thousands of people. All the workers living in the suburbs of Paris had flocked there to get a last glimpse of this leader and writer. Perhaps no other French writer had evoked such respect, such love and was so mourned by the people. For them this thin and weak, pale and tall man with curved shoulders, who had received the gift of tuberculosis from the cold and moist trenches during the First World War, who had raised his voice against barbarism in his novel *Le feu*, was not only a powerful writer but also the symbol of the struggle of revolutionary humanity and of the hopes of a bright future.

At the time, a storm had been raised by André Gide's transmutation in the literary world of Paris. Gide's position was then very high in French literature. Though outside the country, Romain Rolland, Anatole France and Marcel Proust were recognized as the leading novelists of modern France, for the French literary critics Gide's literary stature compared favourably with them. Indeed, the above mentioned authors (of whom Romain Rolland is the only one still living) were not considered quite so 'absolutely modern' as he. From 1935 onwards, the popularity of Gide increased rapidly. Conservative critics pricked their ears when he participated in the International Congress of Writers. How painful it was for them to see this man, the irregularity and mischievousness of whose philosophy of life excited them and the delicacy of whose style satisfied their dilettantish literary conscience, deliver a speech before the dirty and ragged workers, promising to devote his literary efforts for the cause of the people. They declared that Gide's non-seriousness about his attachment to the popular movement was a counterpart of his philosophy of sin. After the publication of Gide's *Les nouvelles nourritures*, their wrath knew no bounds. In this work Gide, who had always preached individual revolt against conventional morality, and who had held the commission of sin to be necessary for the spiritual perfection and emancipation of man, now accepted the aims and objects of socialism, considering it to be the highest stage of individualism.

A few days after the publication of Gide's book, I had an opportunity to hear a lecture by a renowned French writer, Professor Albert Saroux, on the latest literary trends in Gide's work. The meeting was held in the small hall of the French Progressive Writers' Association. In the same hall was situated the office of the International Literary Centre. The hall could hardly accommodate two hundred people, but on this occasion about three hundred persons had turned up. All the chairs were occupied and many people were standing here and there. Prof. Saroux argued that it was natural for Gide to lean towards socialism, for a man who had devoted all his literary efforts to show the path of emancipation to man through ego and sin, if he were honest, would certainly protest against the suppression of individualism in modern capitalist society; and hence, he would necessarily embrace the philosophy of socialism. In the general discussion that followed Saroux's speech, a well-known conservative critic expressed his disagreement with the latter. For him the new trend in Gide signified the dilution of his art, for Gide had given up the position of an artist and had become a political partisan, which according to him, throttled art.

The great French poet and novelist, Aragon, who was also present in the meeting and participated in the discussion, considered the new trend of Gide to be fortunate both for French literature and for the Popular Front in France. He emphasized, however, that Gide's support for socialism was mainly emotional. He was still distanced from Marxist socialism, the only socialism with a scientific basis. Aragon said it was natural for an artist to approach socialism in this way, but if he did not secure a sound intellectual foundation for his socialist thought he could fall into the mire of conservatism at a crucial time. What a pity that Aragon proved to be correct, and that within a year André Gide left the ranks of progressive writers, imprisoning himself in the dark abyss of individualism.

In this connection I may say something about Aragon. The First World War had disturbed the equilibrium of life, with a consequent effect in literature and art. In Europe a group of writers was formed which rejected the old style, form, sentiments, rationality—in short, almost everything old, and thus carried its art and literature to the limit of absurdity. No one understood their poetry, and their paintings and sculptures were meaningless. This movement was called Dadaism and Paris was its centre. Aragon was a young poet of the Dada group but he extricated himself from this 'absolute' revolt and created a place for himself in the front rank of modern French poets.

He made a trip to the Soviet Union, and saw with his own eyes the construction of socialist society. New dams which produced electricity, new factories, mechanized agriculture, a ruling class of workers and peasants and the continuous development of knowledge and arts—these phenomena were for Aragon the highest point of romanticism. He felt it to be the only means by which human spirit could be liberated from the slavery of dead matter, permitting one to breathe in the atmosphere of liberty. His poems about the Soviet Union were famous throughout France. Even those who were not socialists could not but appreciate the sincerity, the innovations in expression and the passion behind these poems.

During my stay in Paris I found Aragon taking a leading part in the progressive movements of French writers and intellectuals. This handsome poet and novelist of average stature and slim body was a very effective speaker. A still more surprising fact about him was his exceptional organizational ability. He was the secretary of the Association of French Writers and also worked in the newly established office

These young men are born in a nation that has lost its values and is living in [. . .] darkness. Products of a hybrid culture, they are vainly trying to evolve a philosophy of life. **A Night in London** *gives a glimpse into the minds and hearts of these unfortunate youths; they are so like the students one meets in the University towns of England and round Gower Street and Bloomsbury.*
—**Shaista Suhrawardy Ikramullah**

of the International Writers' Association. He was very popular among French workers and yet there was a place for him in the most sophisticated and the most exclusive literary circles of Paris.

A common French acquaintance introduced me to Aragon. Within a few minutes we were talking freely and without reserve. Aragon spoke to me for a long time about Indian literature. I told him about the Progressive Writers' Association and said that we had also proposed to start this movement in India. I asked Aragon about his organizational experiences in connection with the French and the International Writers' Associations. I still remember his laughter and the peculiar French manner in which he shrugged his shoulders and said: 'Don't ask that! No other group is more difficult to organize than the writers. Every writer wants an exclusive path for himself. Even then we must continue our efforts. The conditions of the modern world are forcing writers to organize themselves for the defence and progress of their art.'

[As I bid Aragon farewell and stepped outside, darkness had settled in. The lights in the streets were shining brightly. My lodgings were at quite a distance. I boarded a bus, whose route made it pass through the cobblestone streets of that most splendid of all Parisian marketplaces known as the Grand Boulevard. There is perhaps no better place in the world for understanding the meaning of the expression 'in full swing'. In decorating the doors of their shops, cafés, restaurants, cinemas and theatres with an abundance of lights, the French had made every night festive. And then there was a fair bit of activity here as well—people thronged the cafés along the sidewalks, and here and there well-groomed and beautiful women would come into view. Life seemed pleasant. At the same time I was reminded of the female protagonist of Aragon's most recent novel, *Les Cloches de Bâle*, which I had then just finished reading. She, too, was a Frenchwoman, whose life was an unsuccessful attempt at attaining the blessing of love. The egotism of her passions and that of the capitalist way of life had crushed a gentle human spirit. And perhaps it was this individual who, as opposed to all the glitter, pomp and show, gave truer expression to France's fettered, yet bustling and vibrant humanity.]

When I left Paris for India autumn had set in. The trees were no longer green, their leaves were already a yellowish-red. A cold breeze was blowing. It appeared as if someone had extracted the heat out of the sunshine, leaving only its light. It was the best season for leaving Europe. [I was to return on an Italian ship and therefore had to go to Genoa. The clouds of war had gathered over the atmosphere. The conflict between Italy and Ethiopia had already broken out. Troops could be seen everywhere. Although the ship was destined for India, English and Indian passengers were nowhere to be found. It was felt that, should war break out between England and Italy, we would become the

It is not often that people from both sides of the Indo-Pakistan border get to celebrate something in common. Yet the legacy of Sajjad Zaheer, Marxist thinker, writer and journalist is one that is shared by both countries.
—The Hindu

latter's prisoners of war by virtue of our status as British subjects. Perceiving little difference between a British slave and an Italian prisoner, I did not fret much about this danger; and because I had already purchased a ticket, I thought it fitting that I should travel on board that very same Italian liner.

The ship was desolate. Several Italian workers were bound for Ethiopia by way of Massawa, but remained out of sight. I strolled to and fro along the empty decks by myself, spending most of the time writing [my novella]. Neither blue nor calm, the Mediterranean was turning murky, and somewhat restless too. One day the news came that one of the Italian workers had taken his life by jumping overboard. The ship momentarily came to a halt in mid-ocean, but not a trace was to be found of that poor unfortunate soul's body. Why, after all, had he preferred death over going to Ethiopia and constructing a road for the Italian Empire? The question frequently arose in my mind, but who was there to answer it? My cabin mate was an esteemed official of France's Afghan Embassy, Agha Sahib. He spoke only French and Persian, and so I was the sole person on board with whom he could converse—the two languages understood on the ship being Italian and English. The sorrow of leaving Paris had driven him mad, for it was in that centre of beauty and intoxication that the gentleman had to leave behind his Spanish mistress. And those who awaited him in Kabul were his wife and, by God's grace, two children.

Who could keep a sound mind in such a dilemma? He took some of the burden off his chest by repeatedly pouring out his grievances to me. With whom could I share my sorrow?]

A period of life came to an end, and like every end it was poignant, carrying a pathos of its own. The second and more important period had not yet begun. Hopes and yearnings, schemes and plans were agitating my mind.

[The climate above the Arabian Sea was temperate, and the ocean calm. During the night, in the midst of the darkness on all sides, the reflection of moonlight on the ocean's surface would extend to a great distance, resembling a flickering, silver wave. At this hour the only sound that could be heard was that of water rustling against the ship. Or else, at times, a sorrowful Persian lament would sound from my Afghan friend's gramophone:

Don't fall in love, the lover is unfortunate.
Sometimes seeing and at other times losing
sight is a hardship.]

1940

(Originally published in Urdu as 'Yaden' in *Naya Adab* [January-February, 1941], Zaheer's 'Reminiscences' offers a unique glimpse into the author's intellectual and literary development, as well as the origins of the Progressive Writers' Association. The essay used is Khalique Naqvi's abridged translation of the piece, which first appeared in *Indian Literature* [Bombay] 2 [1952], pp. 47-57. The translation has been modified and supplemented by Bilal Hashmi to reflect the original more closely.)

A Night in London [gives] a picture of the life of a section of Indians whose feelings have hitherto not been discussed by any writer [. . .] the reading of which gives the same quality of satisfaction as the reading of poetry or listening to music. It has a quality of terseness, of reality which was so far lacking in Urdu fiction [. . .] [I]t makes one hopeful about the future of the Urdu novel.

—**Shaista Suhrawardy Ikramullah**

The Making of a
Revolutionary

Mulk Raj Anand

Sunday afternoon in the early thirties in London.

The fashionable muffler of New College, Oxford, adorned his neck. He wore a smart navy blue serge suit. His pale face glowed with excitement as he waved the magazine *Bharat* for sale on the outer fringe of a mammoth meeting addressed by the first communist member of the British Parliament, Shapurji Saklatvala in the vast maidan of Hyde Park. He offered me a copy with a gentle smile. I snatched it impetuously and paid the shilling.

'You are Mulk Raj Anand?' he said in a mellifluous Lucknow accent.

'And you are?'

'Sajjad Zaheer,' he answered. 'I saw you yesterday in Krishna Menon's India League Office.'

We shook hands.

Being a Khalifa to most Indian students, by virtue of having stayed on in London to write novels after my researches in philosophy, I enjoyed the status of an old hand in intellectual and political matters. And I asked Sajjad Zaheer to come and have tea with me. The voice of Saklatvala was becoming across the park, and had out the other Hyde Park orators out of business. But we knew the things 'Sak' was saying; and, having already had our familiar feelings confirmed, we went towards the Express Dairy near Marble March.

I had heard the sensation caused, in the Urdu circles of northern India, by the collection of pieces brought together by Sajjad Zaheer under the title *Angarey*. So I asked him if he could lend me a copy of this book.

'I have been longing to meet you and the other writers in this anthology,' I said.

'But we have read *Untouchable*—it is the rage of the Majlis members in Oxford!' Sajjad Zaheer said. 'Why can't we form an organization of writers—of progressive writers?'

'Sajjad Zaheer Sahib,' I said. 'Your thoughts and mine are running parallel. But most of our friends seem only to be interested in themselves, or in intrigues against Krishna Menon. Every Indian intellectual, especially in London, denigrates the other. How can they be brought together in an organization?'

'I will try to get the Urdu writers together,' he said. 'Incidentally, people call me Bunne . . . that is my nickname . . .'

'Bunne' I repeated. 'I am Mulk to everyone.'

'Let us go to a pub instead of the Express Dairy,' Bunne suggested.

I had heard the sensation caused, in the Urdu circles of northern India, by the collection of pieces brought together by Sajjad Zaheer under the title *Angarey*. So I asked him if he could lend me a copy of this book.

That was my first meeting with Sajjad Zaheer, alias 'Bunne' or 'Bunne Bhai' as I came to call him later. And I was drawn to him, especially because, since I had known the poet Iqbal in Lahore, and had sought out Premchand on one of my trips to Uttar Pradesh the previous year, I had not met any other Urdu writer of my own generation from that area, though I had already met Taseer and several other Punjabi writers of Urdu at the house of Sir Abdul Qadir in the West End of London. I was impressed by his gracefulness, the slow movements of his body, and his spontaneous warmth oozing from a gentle face. And I was heartened that this obviously rich young student from Oxford had come specially to hear Saklatvala. I was to learn later from him that quite a few sons of bourgeois families from India had joined the October Club, in the University of Oxford, where I had once spoken.

> I was impressed by his gracefulness, the slow movements of his body, and his spontaneous warmth oozing from a gentle face.

By the time I met Bunne again, he had been to Paris to see some of his friends in the Sorbonne. I remember that Dr J.C. Ghosh, who was a lecturer in English literature in Oxford, and he came together to my room in Bloomsbury, and it was suggested that I should draw up a manifesto for our proposed writers' organization. Bunne had also called Taseer to my place and soon there was a loud knock at my door. I threw down the key and the fat, rather overpowering, personality of this compatriot from Lahore entered.

'So this is Bloomsbury!' Taseer said, with an implied reference to the fact that I had no bed but had spread a mattress, Indian style, on the floor and covered it with a phulkari which my mother had given me from her previous stock during my last visit home.

I went into the little kitchen to make tea and began to sweat from my discomfiture at the typical Government College, Lahore, attitude towards the poor. I recalled how ashamed I had felt of my father's trousers which my mother had altered for me to wear when I went to see a cricket match between Government College, Lahore, and Khalsa College, Amritsar. Most of the students of the Government College, Lahore, being the sons of rich well-placed parents, sported blazers and grey flannel trousers, made by Ranken & Co., whose grandiose premises in Mall Road inspired an awe which I had never been able to surmount. Quite a few of them rode on motor bicycles. And Professor A.S. Bokhari, wearing a bow tie above his immaculate suit, had been pointed out to me by my guardian from Amritsar, Professor M.L. Bhatia, as a model of what a writer should be like. I had then disdained going to buy vegetables for my mother, and I had insisted that one of my eldest brother's hockey blazers be cut to my size; as also I had stopped going to the shops of my cousins, the coppersmiths, for an occasional chat, preferring to go to the railway station with my seniors, Syed Hassan and Trilochan Singh, to drink tea in the English-style First Class dining room of Amritsar Railway. I had begun to look down on all dhoti-clad people, and concentrated on English literature to the exclusion of Urdu and Persian poetry. All this had changed when my mother fell ill and asked me to fetch the doctor. I had then realized that though illiterate, she was my mother, that she was an Indian and so was I, and nothing would make me into an Englishman, not even powder and paint. After I came to London, I and two other Indian students had been beaten by three blacklegging English students outside Euston Square Metro Station, because we backed the general strike called by Cooke on behalf of miners. I had given up the University College, London, blazer. I wore a corduroy suit, grew my hair long, cooked for myself and lived on the little money I could earn as a writer of reviews and articles for the British literary magazines.

Bunne's Oxford blazer I could understand, because it had become worn with use, but Taseer's brown Bond Street suit and pats on the shoes irritated me. Dr Ghosh's bald head and his old suit seemed quite congenial.

'Are there going to be any pastries?' Taseer called out aloud to me as I was just brewing the tea.

'Only short bread biscuits!' I answered. And I brought in the lovely old Chinese lacquer tray, which I had purchased cheap in Caledonian market.

'There is no doubt, he has got taste,' Dr Ghosh said. 'Where did you get those Kangra miniatures?'

'Oh—odds and ends, you know! I sell fat

hunting books I get for review and buy Indian remnants from antique shops, because I am trying to rediscover India.'

'That already gives us the cue for our manifesto,' Bunne said in his low soft voice, 'rediscovery of India—of our Indian culture . . .'

'Rediscovery and Renaissance,' I insisted, not revival à la [Abdur Rahman] Chugtai, the pupil of Abanindranath Tagore! Neither in painting nor in literature must we have revivalism. The dead past can't come back. 'We must be contemporary and face the problems of our time.'

'Bravo!' said Dr Ghosh. 'We agree.'

'But what is wrong with my friend Chugtai,' asked Taseer.

'I don't know art,' Bunne said. 'But isn't he a revivalist?'

Dr Ghosh jeered at the long fingers and almond eyes of the revivalist paintings. The discussion became highly charged, as I supplemented what he said with my own theory that the Bengalis of the nineties, and pre-first world war, were like the Pre-Raphaelites. Taseer was stubborn in the defence of Chugtai. And the discussion was prolonged. The tea was nearly forgotten. The short bread biscuits remained uneaten. There was tension in the room in spite of the mellow twilight. Only Bunne sipped the tea.

'What about the manifesto?' Bunne said.

'Three people can't write anything together,' I said. 'One of us should draft it. Taseer should do the first draft . . .'

. . . [A] good book viewed simply as literature, with realistic characterization, convincing dialogue, and vivid descriptive power.

—Ralph Russell

'How wise you are!' said Taseer.

'Well,' I said, to taunt Taseer, 'I am not such a fool as I look.'

This made for a laugh.

'Let Dr Ghosh try a draft,' Bunne said in his role as a reconciler. And we all agreed.

———

Dr Ghosh did produce a draft in about a month or so. This was adequate but wanting in depth. And, during our discussion of the document, I witnessed a transformation in all of us.

Our friendship seemed to have matured in spite of our differences of opinion.

Also, we had begun to explore the meaning of literature in terms of our love for our people, almost as though there had come about a 'spiritual' conversion from the bourgeois, the petit bourgeois, and the feudalist outlooks, to the acceptance of Indians as human beings of, and despite their shortcomings, weakness and defaults. We began to understand how alien rule had ignored our languages, suppressed our cultures, and won over their allies among our forefathers to false values of snobbery, money, contempt and cynical betrayal of humanness. The Imperialists had first left the people ignorant, exploited them and insulted them, then they had dubbed them stupid, filthy and unfit to be human . . .

Again, we realized that, apart from our romantic gestures, only a few of us had the experience of the suffering of our people, and thus we would have to make our words into acts, that is to say, live the thoughts we believed in before we could consider ourselves worthy of the struggle for liberation. And this would involve efforts to free ourselves from so many of our own failings.

Myself, I was not only born in a poor lower middle-class household, but I had to run away from home, with the help of my mother and Dr Iqbal to undertake research in philosophy, because my father beat my mother for my going to jail in the Gandhi movement. And after I had been urged by conscience to write a long confession, I had still felt the need to go back to India, from my exile, to Gandhiji's ashram in Ahmedabad, to deepen my awareness of the struggle, to simplify my life, and to clean latrines as part of my vow, before I could rewrite my first novel, *Untouchable*. As I had, therefore, had to cut out my own narcissisms to a large extent, I could bring myself more directly on the manifesto.

What was wrong with Dr Ghosh's draft was this very lack, of the self-exiled intellectual of actual experience of people in our country. The abstract idea of freedom was there, but he did not know it really felt like this to be born a poet among the Harijans who were not given the opportunity to go to school. And if I understood Sajjad Zaheer, he meant to evoke the new consciousness of those who had never entered literature.

In Taseer's case, there was revealed an

And if I understood Sajjad Zaheer, he meant to evoke the new consciousness of those who had never entered literature.

uncanny knowledge of the lower middle class but an idealization of their faults. And he had to throw off the influence of I.A. Richards, Quiller, Couch and Eliot, whose critical theories of literature he admired, as a base for raising our literature to higher levels. He had forgotten Muhammad Iqbal.

Bunne, in spite of being the son of the ex-lord Chief Justice of the high court of Oudh, came nearest to me. There seemed to have been already a conversion in him from the exalted upper-class status to affiliation with the people, when he joined the October Club. And, as he lived in close contact with the lower middle class intelligentsia of Oudh, there had accrued to him a genuine awareness of the long pain of the decaying but cultured folk. His mother came from a village in Jaunpur, he told me. So though he could not mock at the failings of his friends, he expressed a kind of holy anger which was near to the core of the single-hearted struggle which we wished to launch in the realm of the spirit.

In my private conversations with him, I felt that the process of transformation in him was not complete, though it was more tense in him than in Dr Ghosh and Taseer. And, as he shared with me his inner feelings more completely than our other two friends, I could appreciate his difficulties.

Luckily, I was in no position to patronize him. And I could indulge his weakness. For instance, he was always late for appointments. His life in a big house, and New College, Oxford, had given him a certain number of

In my private conversations with him [Sajjad Zaheer], I felt that the process of transformation in him was not complete ...

preferences, like a few preoccupations, such as his daily three-hour siesta, which he was not to give up till the long painful experience of active work in the Indian struggle brought him face to face with himself and others, one at the same time. He had, he was to tell me, been to a sanatorium a few years ago, and the doctors had advised a compulsory siesta in the afternoon. He had perhaps been too near the shadows to forget death. And, I knew it might take a long time for him to discover that in words and in actions, that is to say, in creative labour, there is always possible the obliterations of fear, and loneliness and personalism.

But I learnt to accept most of his narcissistic habits with a raucous Punjabi humour, as in fact, everyone including his relations had learnt to do.

The important thing is that, already in the early thirties, he had begun to pursue his creative activities, along with active work with people, especially Indian students and writers, and had brought quite a few of them away from feudal habits, to heighten awareness of the implications of change.

Perhaps the possibilities of deep connection with our contemporaries was rendered easy because until then the status of the Indian student in Oxford and Cambridge was that of a colonial, even if he or she came from a rich household in India. If such students had not suffered any wounds of humiliation in India because their fathers were collaborationists with the alien rulers, the superior attitude of the aristocratic and

> **The important thing is that, already in the early thirties, he had begun to pursue his creative activities, along with active work with people . . .**

conservative students in the two old universities made for the awareness of those nuances of discrimination which are built into the British class society. I don't think there was any Indian student of the three or four generations, whom I know in Oxford and Cambridge, who did not become a nationalist at the very least during his sojourn in Great Britain. Maybe the period of the rise of fascism and the cruelties it perpetrated, as well as the betrayal of imperialist democracies of the peoples of Europe and their continued domination of Asia and Africa until after the Second World War, was too transparent a mirror not to reflect the nature of our enemies, of the enemies of our promise and fulfilment.

The manifesto of the Progressive Writers' Association was passed in the basement of Nanking Restaurant off Charing X Road in London, at one of our monthly meetings.

The importance of this paper by which we vowed lay not in its perfection of analysis, or description, or definition of the cultural situation in India, but in the metamorphosis from the fatalism of the part of the acceptance of the here and the now and the ultimate belief in the many freedoms.

The spirit of togetherness, of unity, was sought to be strengthened, even among writers of different opinions, on the basis of shared values.

Also, though some of us were living in the garrets of Bloomsbury, we felt the need, through this manifesto, to shift our abode from Great Britain to India itself, so that we

> I don't think there was any Indian student of the three or four generations, whom I know in Oxford and Cambridge, who did not become a nationalist at the very least during his sojourn in Great Britain.

could penetrate deeply into the lives of our own human beings and try to create a literature, with concrete characters, in full confrontation with themselves and their human situation.

Our work in the political struggle against fascism intensified our passion. But there were certain questions of influence, like the effect which the 'language of the night' of James Joyce's *Work in Progress* were having on writings of our colleagues. This could only be solved by reverting back to our own languages as they were being spoken by our people.

There were many implications of the Progressive Writers' Manifesto which Sajjad Zaheer and I discussed in those days.

There were many implications of the Progressive Writers' Manifesto which Sajjad Zaheer and I discussed in those days.

One of them was the need for self-criticism, the inquiry into how far, and to what extent, our love of classics was for the use of technique or for source materials? I suggested that we should define our attitude about cultural heritage and assert that we could only take those things from the past which have relevance for our own time and put the rest in the library shelves.

Also, how different was to be our literature from the current bourgeois and feudalist literature? We were not being adolescent in mocking and exposing only, when satire had to be used to create the will to change the superstitious people to rationality, to questioning the dead habits and to the new light of the renaissance.

And what about the cadres for the creation of the advanced literature, men and women who would raise the level of awareness of our unhappy people? Where were they to be found?

We decided that most of these questions could only be settled in India. So Sajjad Zaheer decided that he would finish his Bar exams soon, go back and call a convention of All-India Progressive Writers. I was to return a little later.

I remember with what devotion Sajjad Zaheer pursued his legal studies after this resolution was made. His laziness disappeared. He began to keep appointments on time. And his utterance became clearer, so that he could speak to large audiences without faltering, or hesitations and inhibitions, unlike in the days when I had first met him.

Certainly, the manifesto had began the process of transformation in him. And he duly returned to India soon after . . .

He wrote to me from the midst of the All-India Progressive Writers' Conference, held in Lucknow, 1936, under the presidentship of Premchand. The response to the conference had been enthusiastic. The bulk of the young intelligentsia had rallied behind the declaration.

And soon I was to come and meet in person Majaz, Jafri, Sibte Hassan, Amrit Rai, Ehtesham Hussain, Firaq Gorakhpuri, Ahmed Ali, Abdul Aleem, Sumitra Nandan Pant, P.C. Gupta, Hiren Mukherji, Bishnu Dey and many others whom Sajjad Zaheer had brought together into the fold of this movement.

I stayed in Wazir Manzil, a big rambling house in Butlerjung, Lucknow, as a guest of the Zaheer family for nearly a year. Bunne and I made frequent journeys to almost all parts of India, particularly to Allahabad to work with Jawaharlal Nehru, writing memoranda on various things for Panditji.

I found that Bunne was much loved in his household. In fact, he exercised a pervasive influence by the example of his dedicated life. His father, Sir Wazir Hassan, told everyone to call him 'Syed Wazir Hassan' and not 'Sir Wazir Hassan'. His mother, lovingly called Bubu, was concerned to see him married, so that his children would also be like him. His brothers had great respect for him, in spite of their differences in political outlook. His sister-in-law took pride in preparing special dishes for him when he came back from his tours.

During the next decade, Sajjad Zaheer was to remain, whether he was in jail or out of it, the hub of the Progressive Writers' Movement.

Specially I remember meeting the whole clan on the Id day, when about 50 members came to greet his father and mother.

We held the Second All-India Progressive Writers' Conference in Calcutta in 1938, at which we got Rabindranath Tagore to preside. Sajjad Zaheer and I found ourselves touring all over India to gather support for our movement. And we met warm friendship from writers of almost all the major languages.

During the next decade, Sajjad Zaheer was to remain, whether he was in jail or out of it, the hub of the Progressive Writers' Movement.

I got marooned in the UK where I had returned briefly in early 1939, because the

Second World War was started a year before I had anticipated it. So we were out of contact for seven long years.

Meanwhile, the intensification of the liberation movement had brought Jawaharlal very near to us. Sajjad Zaheer worked closely with him in the A.I.C.C. office, in Allahabad, and was much beloved of Panditji. He was also put in the same jail as Jawaharlal later. And he wrote a letter telling me of the keen interest which Nehru was taking in the renascent ideas of the young. Another old friend of course, who was in jail with him, was Kanwar Brajesh Singh of Kalakankar.

I devoted myself during the first three war years to the writing of my novel *The Sword and the Sickle*, the third volume of my trilogy. This was placed in Kalakankar and narrated the abortive spontaneous struggle of the peasants of Oudh against the Talukdars. I dedicated this book to Sajjad Zaheer, as the first draft had been done when I lived with him in Kalakankar, and Wazir Manzil, Lucknow, and in Lahore. That dedication is my tribute to the inspiration, love and hospitality, which he and his family gave me.

We were together again after the war in Bombay. This was a testing time, because we knew that the British would quit India but leave us divided on the basis of religion.

The hopeful thing was that Sajjad Zaheer had succeeded in keeping the Urdu intelligentsia in a genuine solidarity against communalism. We met every week in the Deodhar Hall near the Opera House of Bombay, and there was a burst of fresh

... we knew that the British would quit India but leave us divided on the basis of religion.

poetry and prose from new poets and novelists like Kaifi Azmi, Rajinder Singh Bedi, Ismat Chughtai, Majrooh Sultanpuri, Shailendra and others. The older writers Krishan Chander, Jafri and Ahmad Abbas, continued to write maturely.

In 1947, the partition of India and Pakistan plunged us in abysmal gloom. We had to accept the bloodbath and the separation from our friends, like Faiz Ahmed Faiz.

At the juncture, Sajjad Zaheer decided to go, as soon as possible, to Pakistan and to work for goodwill among the old freedom fighters, as well as to try and work with the new intelligentsia for the common cause of Indian and Pakistani people—bread and soul.

We saw him off at the then little Santa Cruz aerodrome of Bombay and knew that he would have to go underground on arrival in Karachi, as the power groups, which had taken over in the newly founded state, were the old vested interest of landlordism and reaction.

And so it turned out. Sajjad Zaheer lived and worked mostly in hiding. And he rallied quite a few of the advance guard around him.

But soon, he was accused, with Faiz Ahmed Faiz and some others, of trying to upset the duly constituted Government of Pakistan. The trial went on for a few years, while he was lodged in a jail in Balochistan. Only world opinion, which worked hard to intercede on his behalf, secured his release after a few years.

Jawaharlal Nehru, who had tremendous affection for Sajjad Zaheer, intervened

> Sajjad Zaheer decided to go [. . .] to Pakistan and to work for goodwill among the old freedom fighters, as well as to try and work with the new intelligentsia for the common cause of Indian and Pakistani people . . .

personally with the Pakistan government to secure his return to India.

In 1958, Nehru inspired us to organize the First Conference of the Asian Writers in New Delhi. In this task, I and Sajjad Zaheer had all the writers with us except a few of those who were the enemies of promise. The reunion of all those intellectuals, who had been separated in different countries of Asia by imperialism, was one of the happiest tasks achieved in India. At this conference, the Soviet writers gave an invitation to the next conference to be held in Tashkent.

In 1958, therefore, we foregathered on the banks of the Amu River, in Uzbekistan, in what was to be the first Afro-Asian Writers' Conference. The lush hospitality and the generosity of the Soviet intelligentsia made it possible to initiate a worldwide movement from Tashkent, which was to spread all over Asia, Africa, and even to make itself felt in Latin America.

Since then, the Afro-Asian Writers' Conference has met every three years in a different country. The second conference was in Cairo, where the late President Nasser played host. The third gathering was in Beirut, where the Lebanese intelligentsia familiarized the Afro-Asian writers with the interior problems of the Arab world, fighting against the occupation of Palestine by the Israel state, with its constant threats of war on the surrounding areas.

In 1970, the honour came to India to organize the fourth Afro-Asian Writers' Conference. Again both Sajjad Zaheer and

Jawaharlal Nehru, who had tremendous affection for Sajjad Zaheer, intervened personally with the Pakistan government to secure his return to India.

myself were able, with the help of Indira Gandhi, to host one of the largest gatherings of intellectuals in New Delhi.

It is not an irony of fate, but perhaps an inevitable fact, that Sajjad Zaheer, who struggled silently but faithfully, for the preservation of our fighting culture against the assaults of commercialism, war and despair, should have died during the session of the 5th Afro-Asian Writers' Conference in Alma Ata amid the love and concern of his many international friends. His death came suddenly and has been a great shock to those who believed that this gentle, quiet and ever-smiling personality was too poised to suffer from tension. Alas! He is no more. And he will not be there to reconcile people of different opinions in the support of big causes. With his going has passed away one of the few intellectuals of our country, committed to the service of the disinherited, the poorest of the poor, and the most downtrodden. He was an example of utmost decency in personal relations. He was one of the most talented and sensitive socialist–humanists of our country.

With his going has passed away one of the few intellectuals of our country, committed to the service of the disinherited, the poorest of the poor, and the most downtrodden.

I feel an empty space around me, as he will not spontaneously recite to me one of his new poems—because he will not be there at home when I go to see him.

But I know his words are part of the inspiration of our generation—perhaps of the new younger generations as well.

(Originally published as 'Some Reminiscenes of Sajjad Zaheer' in *Lotus: Afro-Asian Writings* 26 [October-December 1975], pp. 44–51.)

Manifesto of the Indian Progressive Writers' Association, London

It is the duty of Indian writers to give expression to the changes taking place in Indian life and to assist the spirit of progress in the country.

Radical changes are taking place in Indian society. Fixed ideas and old beliefs, social and political institutions are being challenged. Out of the present turmoil and conflict, a new society is arising. The spirit of reaction, however, though moribund and doomed to ultimate decay, is still operative and is making desperate efforts to prolong itself.

It is the duty of Indian writers to give expression to the changes taking place in Indian life and to assist the spirit of progress in the country.

Indian literature, since the breakdown of Classical culture, has had the fatal tendency to escape from the actualities of life. It has tried to find a refuge from reality in spiritualism and idealism. The result has been that it has produced a rigid formalism and a banal and perverse ideology. Witness the mystical–devotional obsession of our literature, its furtive and sentimental attitude towards sex, its emotional exhibitionism and its almost total lack of rationality. Such literature was produced particularly during the past two centuries, one of the most unhappy periods of our history, a period of disintegrating feudalism and of acute misery and degradation for the Indian people as a whole.

It is the object of our association to rescue literature and other arts from the priestly, academic and decadent classes in whose hands they have degenerated so long; to bring the arts into closest touch with the people; and to make them the vital organs which will register the actualities of life, as well as lead us to the future.

While claiming to be the inheritors of the best traditions of Indian civilization, we shall criticize ruthlessly, in all its political, economic and cultural aspects, the spirit of reaction in our country; and we shall foster through interpretative and creative work (with both native and foreign resources) everything that will lead our country to the new life for which it is striving. We believe that the new literature of India must deal with the basic problems of our existence today—the problems of hunger and poverty, social backwardness and political subjection, so that it may help us to understand these problems, and through such understanding help us to act.

With the above aims in view, the following resolutions have been adopted:

(1) The establishment of organizations of writers to correspond to the various linguistic zones of India; the coordination of these organizations by

While claiming to be the inheritors of the best traditions of Indian civilization, we shall criticize ruthlessly, in all its political, economic and cultural aspects, the spirit of reaction in our country ...

Talking of the progressive movement in Urdu literature and its contribution to secularism and composite culture formation in India, the name of its pioneer, Syed Sajjad Zaheer, cannot be overlooked.

—*The Tribune*

holding conferences, publishing of magazines, pamphlets, etc.

(2) To co-operate with those literary organizations whose aims do not conflict with the basic aims of the Association.

(3) To produce and to translate literature of a progressive nature and of a high technical standard, to fight cultural reaction; and, in this way, to further the cause of Indian freedom and social regeneration.

(4) To strive for the acceptance of a common language (Hindustani) and a common script (Indo–Roman) for India.

(5) To protect the interests of authors; to help authors who require and deserve assistance for the publication of their works.

(6) To fight for the right of free expression of thought and opinion.

(This manifesto has been signed by Dr Mulk Raj Anand, Dr K.S. Bhat, Dr J.C. Ghose, Dr S. Sinha, M.D. Taseer, S.S. Zaheer.)

All communications to be addressed to:

Dr M.R. Anand, 32 Russell Square, London, W.C.I

London, 1935